BLOWN OUT OF THE WATER!

"Up there!" one of the passengers near Nancy yelled, pointing.

Nancy looked up and spotted a trio of black-clad gunmen occupying positions on the upper decks. They carried assault rifles and suddenly opened fire.

Nancy ducked behind an open door leading to a companionway. She looked for Bess and found her hidden behind a table a few feet away. Nancy ran to her, crouching for cover, and caught sight of a movement from above. She saw one of the gunmen aiming a gun with a long tube for a barrel right at them.

"Move!" she told Bess, grabbing her friend's shoulder and yanking her into motion.

The tube jumped in the man's hands, and Nancy heard a large object whiz by and out over the railing. Scanning the scene on the water, she saw what happened to the two-masted yacht that took the gunman's fire. In an instant the boat burst into a ball of flaming debris. . . .

Nancy Drew & Hardy Boys SuperMysteries

Available from ARCHWAY Paperbacks

A NANCY AND HARDY DREW AND BOYS SUPER MYSTERY™

OPERATION: <u>TITANIC</u>

Carolyn Keene

AN ARCHWAY PAPERBACK
Published by POCKET BOOKS
New York London Toronto Sydney Tokyo Singapore

This book is a work of fiction. Names, characters, places and incidents are products of the author's imagination or are used fictitiously. Any resemblance to actual events or locales or persons, living or dead, is entirely coincidental.

AN ARCHWAY PAPERBACK *Original*

An Archway Paperback published by
POCKET BOOKS, a division of Simon & Schuster Inc.
1230 Avenue of the Americas, New York, NY 10020

Copyright © 1998 by Simon & Schuster Inc.
Produced by Mega-Books, Inc.

ISBN: 0-671-00737-8

First Archway Paperback printing February 1998

10 9 8 7 6 5

Cover art by Franco Accornero

Printed in the U.S.A.

IL 6+

OPERATION: TITANIC

Chapter

One

WE'VE GOT HIM!"

"You're sure?" Nancy Drew's bright blue eyes shone with excitement from the front seat of the van.

Tommy Buskirk acted disappointed. "You doubt me?"

Tommy was one of the many men Nancy's best friend, Bess Marvin, had developed a crush on in her unending quest for true love. While Bess hadn't found her prince, Nancy had made a friend—a friend who was a whiz at computers and hacking.

"I never doubted you for a minute, Tommy," Nancy replied with an impish grin.

Nancy, Tommy, FBI Agent Vince Tarkington, and radio producer Jason Watson had been sitting for hours in a dreary parking lot on Chicago's West Side. Through the seemingly ceaseless late-summer rain, they watched the Bon Homme apartment complex.

"Well, I still have a few doubts," Agent Tarkington stated. He sat behind Tommy, wearing a dark suit and tie. He was dressed like almost every other FBI agent Nancy had ever met.

Tarkington was observing the cellular phone tracking device, or trigger fish, that Tommy held. The agent's pistol gleamed in the shoulder holster under his open jacket when he leaned forward.

Jason, who was sitting with Tarkington and behind Tommy, caught Nancy's eye and looked at her hopefully. The two had known each other since they were kids. Jason was no longer the geek he had been as a child. He had found his calling as the producer of radio WUUL's late-night show with the phenomenally popular DJ Virgyl Laser. It was Jason who had called Nancy to ask her to help them find out who was scamming their cruise ticket giveaway on Virgyl's show.

Nancy and Tommy had been following their suspect, Trey Carter, for three days. They knew where he was, but had yet to catch him.

As Nancy glanced back at Tarkington, she began feeling nervous. The stakeout had been her idea, and her father, attorney Carson Drew, had contacted the Federal Bureau of Investigation to make it happen.

Tarkington's superior had told him that Nancy

Drew was someone to listen to. If she said this was the night to catch Carter, it was worth their time and energy, he said, to send in some agents.

The hours they'd sat waiting, however, had started to erode Nancy's confidence. Tommy had carefully tracked the names and Internet accounts used in the scam to the apartment of one Herman Giger, an alias of Carter's. Still, Nancy couldn't shake her fear that they might be on a wild-goose chase.

"See?" Tommy said, pointing to the columns of telephone numbers that scrolled across the glowing monitor. "A number of cell phone lines originate from this apartment complex, and Carter is starting to trap the lines at the radio station."

"Turn on the radio, Jason," Nancy said, her voice expressing both her tension and her excitement.

Jason turned it on and cranked up the volume. Virgyl Laser's smoky baritone filled the van.

"Keep those phones ringing, chums and chumettes," Virgyl commanded, "because tonight lucky listener number one hundred and four is going to win the final ticket giveaway for the cruise that's going to witness the *Titanic* being raised. For all of you listeners who are fuzzy about history, that's the ship they said couldn't sink but did."

"Must we listen to this?" the FBI agent asked. No one answered, and no one turned off the radio.

"Okay, I promised to say the leader of this expedition's name on the air, and here it is: Walter Welsch. He's the billionaire everyone's so crazy about. That's right, the guy on the cover of *V.I.P.* magazine. It's his money that's being used to raise the *Titanic,* and the cruise is on his ship, the *Hampton.*

"And you could be there, if you are lucky caller number one oh four. Better than that, there are going to be—count 'em—one hundred and three *loo-ooo-sers* before you!"

Virgyl began his countdown. None of the callers escaped being heckled as the DJ hung up on one after another of them between Top Forty songs.

"Virgyl's in rare form tonight," Jason said.

"Sure is," Nancy answered, not enjoying listening to Virgyl's bombastic and obnoxious chatter.

"It sounds as if Virgyl Laser is trying to pick a fight," Tommy said.

Jason gave a crooked grin. "At least a dozen every night. It's part of his charm."

"Caller seventy-two," Virgyl said, a sneer in his voice. "You're on the air, pal, and let me be the first to tell you that you're a *loo-ooo-ser!*"

Canned jeering trumpeted over the radio waves. The DJ cut off the caller's angry response in midsyllable with practiced ease.

"Do you really think Carter is in there?" Jason asked, studying the apartment building.

Nancy nodded. "Jason, stay cool. I wouldn't

be here if I didn't *know* he was in there," she said with more assurance than she felt. "He's gotten overly confident and hasn't covered his tracks very well." Nancy tried to sound confident.

"Trey Carter has scammed a lot of radio contests before WUUL," Nancy continued. "There was a Corvette giveaway in Miami six years ago."

After doing her research, Nancy knew his history better than almost anyone. So far, four sets of the cruise tickets he'd won had turned up on the Internet for sale.

The fact that the tickets showed up on the Web sites hadn't surprised anyone, since scalpers had been selling tickets on-line for years. But the WUUL tickets were for special cabins, so tracing them had been easy.

"Carter's lighting up the telephone switchboard at the radio station, closing out all the incoming calls but his own," Tommy announced without looking up from his trigger fish. "He must have installed preset traps on the station lines through the phone company's system."

"We have to catch Carter at it," Jason said. "Otherwise the charges won't stick."

"We will," Tarkington said. "If he's there."

Nancy wished the FBI agent would lighten up a little. "He's there," she said once more.

"Caller eighty-four, you're on the air."

"Hello." The voice sounded timid, squeaky.

"That's him," Tommy said with certainty. "He's trying to disguise his voice."

"Can you confirm that the call is coming from inside the apartment complex?" Tarkington asked.

The young computer expert nodded. "You bet."

"Eighty-four," the DJ snarled, "you're just another *loo-ooo-ser!*" The phone connection broke.

"Carter's on again," Tommy said. "I'm showing a different number, but it's logging through the same telephone switch block here at the apartments."

"Caller eighty-five," Virgyl Laser said.

"Rats." This voice was deeper, but Nancy could hear that it was the same person as eighty-four.

"Loo-ooo-ser!" Virgyl Laser declared.

The next six callers came from the apartment complex as well, and all had similar voices.

"He's using at least four different cellular phone lines," Tommy declared. "He's almost there. . . . Bingo! He's got the phone switch box at the radio station completely trapped. No one but Carter can get through to Virgyl now."

"Okay," Tarkington said into the microphone he held that connected him to his men. "Let's close in." He popped open the side door and stepped out into the rain. The butt of his gun filled his hand.

Tarkington opened Nancy's door from the outside. "We're going in to take Herman Giger's apartment."

"Right," Nancy said, "but he isn't necessarily in that apartment. We'll scout around for pay phones. He could be calling from anywhere in the complex."

"Roger," Tarkington answered. By then Tommy and Jason had joined him in the rain. "Be careful," he said, and disappeared into the darkness.

"Caller ninety-four," Virgyl Laser called out mockingly, "you are a *loo-ooo-ser!*"

"Ten more callers," Nancy said, "and we have to find Trey Carter before he gets off the air."

She lifted her jacket collar to keep out the rain. She had come dressed to capture a criminal on a dark, rainy night. She wore a black rain jacket over a black T-shirt and black jeans, her strawberry blond hair hidden under a black watch cap. By the time they'd made it to the main building, Nancy's "waterproof" jacket was soaked through and she felt chilled.

"Where are we going?" Jason asked.

Nancy felt like saying that they were going wherever Trey Carter was. Instead she simply said, "Follow me."

They started off making a circuit of the courtyard at a jog. Three quarters of the way around, Nancy slid to a stop in front of a metal security door. The door read Laundry.

"The laundry probably has pay phones," Tommy said, just before Nancy could voice the same opinion. "He could be calling from inside here."

Nancy tried the door—it was locked. She peered in through the chicken-wire protected pane of glass in the door. The room was a long rectangle with washers running in a double column down the center. Dryers lined the wall to the right opposite windows that overlooked the courtyard.

"Carter wasn't in his room," Tommy said in a low voice.

"How do you know?" Jason demanded.

Tommy opened his palm, revealing a small electronic device. "Police scanner. When Tarkington wasn't looking, I took a peek at the frequency he's using to communicate with the police. I'm hooked in with them."

Nancy shuddered as lightning zigzagged across the sky. In the sudden brilliant light, she saw a tall figure shadowed against the rain-spattered windows of the laundry room. Then it was gone.

Nancy used her cellular phone to call Tarkington "I think Carter's in the buildings' laundry room. And I definitely saw some pay phones in there."

"You've seen him?" The FBI agent sounded tense.

"I saw someone. The laundry is closed and locked. No one should be inside."

"It could be a maintenance man," Tarkington replied.

"A maintenance man would have the lights on," she retorted. "We'll let you know if Carter's inside in just a second." Nancy held the telephone in place with her chin as she fished her lock picks from a pocket.

"Don't go—" Tarkington started to say.

Nancy took the phone from her shoulder and thumbed the mute button as she jiggled the pick in the keyhole. In no time at all, she had pulled open the door and was waving at the others to stay put.

Inside, Nancy flattened herself against the wall next to the door. She couldn't see the phones, but remembered from her brief glimpse that they were in the far corner. She listened intently for a moment before dropping into a low crouch.

After leaving the door slightly ajar, Tommy slipped in beside her. She motioned him to get down.

"Shouldn't we give this a little more thought?" Jason whispered from outside. "Guys?"

He received no answer.

The scent of detergents and cleaners burned Nancy's nose and crept into her throat as she breathed silently. She put the earphone from her portable radio into her ear. It was tuned to WUUL.

Using the line of washers in the center of the room as a defense, Nancy moved forward. She had to navigate a course around the laundry carts on wheels, which were hung with hangers. She didn't want to announce their presence by bumping into one of them.

"Caller one-oh-one," Virgyl Laser said in her ear, "you're with me live, but you're going to wish you were dead, because you are a *loo-ooo-ser!"*

The caller hung up without responding.

Nancy glanced behind her, but Tommy was not there. Her heart pounded in her chest wildly until she realized that Tommy must have taken the other side of the washers. Playing hide-and-seek with someone like Trey Carter wasn't her idea of fun, but she thrived on the rush of adrenaline.

Lightning streaked the sky again, illuminating the room with a sudden intensity. Tommy spoke loudly into the ensuing silence after the crackle of thunder passed. "Carter's gone."

Straightening up, Nancy saw Tommy at the bank of pay phones, a pen-size flashlight in one hand and a pay phone receiver with a cellular phone taped to it in the other. Tommy's light played over the rest, all of them had cellular phones taped to them.

"Not gone," a harsh voice said out of the darkness. "Not yet!"

A chill enveloped Nancy as she saw Trey Carter step from the shadow of the dryers, one arm straight before him and shoulder high. A succession of lightning bolts cracked the sky, revealing the small pistol in his hand. The gun unleashed lightning of its own as Carter pulled the trigger, and the hollow crash of Tommy hitting the empty washers was its rolling thunder.

Carter swung around, bringing his pistol to bear on Nancy.

Nancy dropped, taking cover, as a bullet struck sparks from an open washer lid, slamming it shut.

"Nancy!" Jason yelled, opening the door.

"Get down!" Nancy yelled.

Jason dropped an instant before a bullet dug into the metal door frame where his head had been.

Suddenly the thought occurred to Nancy that there was no way she could explain getting shot to her father. Deadly business like this usually followed Frank and Joe Hardy around. Nancy wished one of the brothers was there now.

Her eyes having adjusted to the dark, Nancy could see Tommy shift slightly on the concrete floor.

"Chums and chumettes," DJ Virgyl Laser whined through her earphone, "you're letting me down. We're only one more *loo-ooo-ser* away from tonight's big winner, and I don't see a single phone line lighting up the switchboard here at WUUL, home of today's hottest music. Come on, don't keep me in suspense."

Virgyl wasn't getting any calls because Carter wasn't calling. He had disappeared from view, but Nancy knew he still had to be in the room.

She inched her way in a crawl over to Tommy, and lifting his arm across her shoulders, helped him into a low crouch.

Tommy moaned softly and put a hand to the side of his head. His face shone pale in the dark.

Nancy yanked the radio from her jacket pocket and cranked up the volume. She flipped the radio away from her, holding on to the earplug.

Blaring rock music filled the laundry as the radio pulled free from the end of the earplug cord. As Carter fired, Nancy yelled "Now!" to Tommy, propelling him down the row of washers toward the door. Jason held it open wide.

The bullet had shattered the radio, and against the sound of the steady rain, Nancy heard Carter come after them.

The sickly light from the lone courtyard lamp revealed no safe cover outside, only the skeletal shape of a jungle gym next to a dented slide.

"The playground!" Nancy yelled to Jason, pointing, and she half carried Tommy toward its meager protection.

Abruptly, Tommy came to a halt at her side and wouldn't—or couldn't—move.

"Come on, Tommy," Nancy cried. Then she saw it, the shadow that separated itself from the darkness not twenty feet ahead.

Nancy's brain instantly registered the dark figure dressed in black. One pinpoint of light reflected off the large pistol in the stranger's gloved hands.

Nancy hit the dirt, dragging Tommy down, and shouted to Jason, but the shadow wasn't focused on them. Unable to stop his forward movement, however, Carter, who was still behind Nancy, ran into the bullets that the stranger fired.

The successive gun flashes revealed the stranger's face—triangular, avocado green, and dominated by huge black lidless eyes—before temporarily blinding Nancy. She blinked several times to get rid of the spots before her eyes, and when she could see again, the other-worldly gunman was gone.

Nancy heard a stampede of feet.

"Are you all right?" Tarkington asked, kneeling beside her.

"Yes," Nancy replied. She turned back toward the laundry room. Jason, standing beside three FBI agents with their weapons drawn, was looking down at Carter's prone body.

"What happened?" Tarkington demanded harshly.

"Someone shot Carter," Nancy said deliberately.

"I kind of figured that out for myself." Tarkington still held his gun. "Did you see who?"

Nancy tried to figure how best to break the news to Tarkington. He wasn't going to like it.

Jason came to her rescue. "Yeah, we saw who shot Carter. But if this guy flees home, I think you're going to have trouble getting him extradited."

Chapter
Two

"Do you know what I need?" Joe Hardy asked his brother, Frank. Joe lounged carelessly in the passenger seat of their van, looking at a collectors' issue of an *X-Guardian, Mutant Avenger for Hire* comic in the glow of a dim flashlight. The garish cover showed a colorfully clad hero battling aliens with ray guns.

"Do you want me to make a comprehensive list?" Frank asked. He kept both hands on the steering wheel of the van, following the tunnel of light on the two-lane road taking them through the dark Massachusetts countryside.

They'd started out early that morning from their home in Bayport but had stopped in Connecticut and then again west of Boston for dinner. Their trip had stretched out an extra four hours.

Joe's blue eyes glinted beneath sun-bleached eyebrows that matched his blond hair. He wore a tangerine tank top and cut-off jeans that revealed the deep tan he'd picked up over the summer. "What I need," he said, "are mutant abilities."

Frank glanced in the rearview mirror and noted the twin headlights that slid into view. At six foot one, he was one inch taller than Joe. At eighteen, he was a year older. His dark brown hair and dark brown eyes were inherited from their father. A more conservative dresser than his brother, Frank wore a short-sleeved denim shirt and khaki shorts with snap-down pockets.

"And what would you do with mutant abilities?" Frank asked.

"The same thing we're doing now. Fight crime." Joe laughed, feeling clever.

Frank and Joe were the sons of Fenton Hardy, a renowned private investigator. As they'd grown up, they'd helped their father with some of his cases, eventually gaining a well-deserved reputation as top detectives on their own.

Their talents had kept them busy almost their whole summer vacation from high school. Their father had used them on a couple of investigations, and they had survived their own adventures as well. They needed a vacation from their vacation, and that was why they were headed for the Wedge Grove Oceanography Institute to visit their friend Eric Cox. Eric had promised them a little swimming, snorkeling, and beach volleyball, plus a whole lot of rest and relaxation.

Frank checked the rearview mirror again. The headlights behind him had closed the gap between the two vehicles, and the car was now back about a hundred yards. Frank put his foot down heavier on the accelerator. The van sped up slightly, momentarily creating distance from the other vehicle, which quickly closed the space to a hundred yards again.

Frank's scalp tightened. Long ago he had learned to pay attention to his subconscious, and he was sensing that, like a moth, the car was drawn to the taillights of the van.

"I can't believe Eric is hooked on these comic books," Joe declared.

"That comic completes his collection of *X-Guardian,* and that's the only thank-you present we've brought him," Frank said, "so you'd better take care of it."

"Okay, okay," Joe said carefully putting the comic away in a protective plastic sheath. "Want a soda?"

"Sure," Frank answered calmly.

Joe released his seat and spun it around to face the rear of the van. He reached down into the cooler their aunt Gertrude had helped them pack that morning and came up with two cans of soda. He didn't turn back around immediately.

"How long has that car been following us?" Joe asked.

"Since you started talking about mutant abilities, or so." Frank was keeping the van at a steady fifty miles per hour, but the distance between the two vehicles had dwindled to fifty yards, now to twenty. The bright lights bored through the back windows of the van.

"We're about seven miles from Wedge Grove," Joe said. "The way I remember the map, there's not much between us and the institute."

"Right," Frank confirmed.

Wedge Grove was located in the southeastern corner of Massachusetts. The oceanography institute compound was relatively isolated on the coast—as isolated as a touristy area could be.

"So either they're in more of a hurry than we are," Joe stated, "or they're interested in us."

Frank pulled the van to the right side of the road to see if the car would pass. The van's headlights disappeared into the patch of night above the curving road. Highway signs warned of a steep drop off and a dangerous curve.

Casually, the trailing vehicle gave a left signal and pulled out into the other lane.

"I make it a late-model Chevy Suburban," Frank said, checking the side mirror. "Do you see a license plate?"

"No."

Frank felt even more uneasy. Only a handful of states didn't require front license plates— Massachusetts was among them.

"It's passing us," Joe said.

Frank kept an eye on the approaching curve in the road. "I'm going to let the Suburban have the road." He put his foot on the brake and started to slow the van.

The Suburban began to roll by, then suddenly it turned directly into their path.

"We're looking at murder now," Special Agent Tarkington announced. "And murder is under the jurisdiction of the local police, not the FBI."

Nancy nodded, but the up and down movement got lost in a shiver that ran through her. It was cold, and she was wet, not to mention a bit shaken from her experiences of the night.

"There's no sign of your alien," the FBI agent continued. His eyes drifted to the white-sheet-covered corpse in the back of the EMT truck.

"He got away," Jason said. "But it looks as if he may have abducted Tommy. Tommy's missing."

Nancy turned around, scanning the wet playground, now eerily lit by arriving police cars. As she stood there trying to call up the moments just before Tommy disappeared, she spotted him jogging weakly back toward them from around the corner of a building.

"He outran me," Tommy gasped. "The guy was a lot faster than I thought."

"You're bleeding," Nancy said, moving forward. She studied the small furrow on Tommy's head that leaked blood down the side of his cheek.

"It's only a flesh wound," he cracked, his face pale. "Isn't that what they say in the movies? But, oh man, do I have a headache."

"You followed the gunman?" Tarkington asked.

Tommy pointed to an alley between buildings. "The guy went through there and then hopped a bus at the corner. There's a shelter there. He was gone before I could get close to him."

"You're sure?" Tarkington asked.

"He was wearing the same clothes," Tommy answered. He held his head. "I've got to sit down somewhere."

Nancy walked him a few short feet to the ambulance that was rolling to a stop. After making sure Tommy was in good hands, Nancy rejoined the FBI agent.

"The man who shot Carter was a professional," Nancy stated.

"I think I'd have to agree." Tarkington readjusted his jacket collar against the still falling rain. "But tell me why you think so."

"Carter was obviously the target," Nancy said. "The man just stepped out of the shadows and fired. No hurry, no hesitation. As if Carter were the only person here."

Tarkington nodded. "I'm sorry you had to witness that."

Nancy was grateful he didn't remind her that he had wanted her to stay in the surveillance van.

A beefy detective trotted up to them with one hand clamped on his fedora to keep it on his head. He had craggy features and a bristly mustache, a fireplug of a man wrapped in a dark green trench coat. "Detective Reynolds, here. I've got some questions about your shooter."

Tarkington nodded.

Nancy crowded closer, while trying not to appear obvious.

"The guy was a pro," the detective declared flatly. "You know what I got here?" He held out a clear plastic evidence bag toward Tarkington.

"Casings," Tarkington answered without looking closely. "Twenty-two caliber, center-fire."

The detective pouted. "You peeked."

Nancy smiled at Detective Reynolds's humor, but Tarkington didn't betray himself with even a glint in his eye.

"I left the brass where it was for your people to pick up," the FBI agent responded.

"I appreciate that," Reynolds said sarcastically. He jammed the evidence bag into his trench coat pocket. "Want to tell me about it?"

"I've already told you all I know, Detective Reynolds," the FBI agent replied.

Reynolds shook his head. "I got a felon shot dead, three measured rounds, and twenty-two caliber casings—a caliber that is favored by a lot of professionals. And I got FBI at the scene. Can you see why I might not think I'm getting it all?"

"You know about the radio scam," Tarkington said.

"Scamming tickets to an ocean cruise isn't exactly something I'd figure a guy could get himself dead over," the detective growled. "I mean, what are they worth? A couple hundred bucks?"

"Two thousand," Jason said defensively. "And that's only direct retail for a comparable trip without the addition of its being the *Titanic* cruise. I've heard some people have paid as much as ten thousand to scalpers for these tickets."

"It's not worth two grand to me, much less ten," the detective said.

Nancy thought that Reynolds had a good point. She'd been puzzling out the basic questions herself: Who would have anything to gain by Carter's death? Who would kill for cruise tickets? And who would know to kill Carter for them?

"The dead man didn't have any tickets on him tonight," Reynolds said. He locked his eyes on Nancy. "And the killer didn't even approach the body, right?"

"Right," Nancy replied. "He didn't."

"Yeah." Reynolds adjusted his trench coat. "Makes no sense. You're going to kill a guy for something, you want to make sure you got it before taking off, right?"

Nancy got the feeling that the detective had deliberately cultivated the slow-thinking, dumb-cop image, but was really pretty sharp.

"So it makes me wonder," Reynolds went on, "whether the killer wasn't protecting something instead."

"You mean protecting the fact that Carter wasn't scamming the radio station on his own," Nancy said.

Reynolds smiled. "Bright girl. My mother warned me to look out for girls like you."

"Your mother," Nancy replied, "was a bright woman."

Reynolds smiled more broadly, which made Nancy like him in spite of his gruff manner.

"Was there anything to make you think that Carter *wasn't* working alone on this gig?" Reynolds asked.

Nancy shook her head. The movement made her realize her hair was plastered to her scalp under her cap.

"How about you, Agent Tarkington?" Reynolds turned to face the FBI man.

"No." Tarkington returned the detective's level gaze. "I got briefed on the situation initially by Ms. Drew and Tommy Buskirk."

"The kid being checked out by the EMTs?"

"Yes, that's Tommy," Nancy answered.

"I pulled Carter's file," Tarkington added. "He'd had partners before, but nobody in particular, and no one lately."

"So, you think he was working by himself?" The detective's eyes narrowed as he asked the question.

"Yes," Tarkington replied, obviously unwilling to elaborate.

Reynolds turned to Jason. "So tell me about the WUUL ticket scam."

In terse sentences, Jason relayed the story of the *Titanic* cruise giveaway tickets showing up on the Internet. "We lucked onto them," he admitted. "The promotional team at WUUL tracked the ticket turnover. Including what came from scalpers. That's when Oscar, the guy in charge of advertising, noticed our tickets on the Web sites. Four straight weeks of them. That was too much of a coincidence."

Reynolds nodded his agreement. He looked at Nancy. "That's when you got involved."

"Yes," Nancy answered. "As soon as Tommy and I identified Trey Carter, we notified the FBI."

"Has anybody checked out the winners of the radio giveaway?" the detective asked.

Jason shook his head. "If WUUL started doing that, the media would be all over them. The raising of the *Titanic* is big news, and we don't want bad publicity."

"The first thing I'm going to want is a list of winners," Reynolds said, jabbing his finger at Jason.

"I don't think the station—" Jason began.

"Just do it," Reynolds commanded. "I'm working a homicide. Your radio station will just have to handle the bad publicity." He handed a cellular phone to Jason. "Call your boss. I want the list on my desk in the morning."

Jason didn't look at all happy; in fact, he looked rather ill, but he took the phone and punched in the number of the radio station.

Reynolds's walkie-talkie beeped at him, and he stepped aside to take the call. When he finished, he spoke directly to Nancy. "You want to come with me? I think we found your alien. I need you to make the ID."

Chapter

Three

THE RIGHT REAR of the Suburban slammed into the front left of the Hardys' van. The impact nearly sent the van spinning out of control as Frank lost hold of the steering wheel. It took him less than a second to tighten his grip again. He slowly pumped the brakes before gently applying increased pressure.

"That was definitely on purpose," Joe said as the van slowed.

The tires along the right side snapped and popped loose gravel from the narrow shoulder fronting the steep drop to a pond below. Glancing through the windshield on his side of the van, Joe saw the tops of bushes and scrub pine.

The Suburban pulled away. For a moment Joe thought it was going to take off, but it quickly reversed and roared back at them. The big utility vehicle slammed into the van again and again. Using the Suburban's greater weight and mass, the driver was having more success this time.

Joe watched as Frank struggled to pull free of the bigger vehicle. As the van teetered at the edge of the drop off, brush whipped at its side in a staccato of brisk blows. The headlights of the van briefly illuminated black water waiting below.

Just when Joe thought they were going to be able to pull free, he heard metal screech against metal as the Suburban slid along the van.

"Look out!" Frank yelled. "He's got a gun!"

Joe glanced to his left and spotted the passenger in the Suburban holding a huge, military-style pistol with both hands. He ducked down in his seat as the bullet shattered the window next to Frank and buried itself in the ceiling. Then Joe felt his stomach rise and fall abruptly as the wheels of the van lifted off the ground. There was a moment of weightlessness as they sailed into the air and plunged over the incline.

A branch slammed into the windshield in front of Joe, sending long, thick cracks across the glass. He braced himself against his seat back and glanced over at Frank.

Brush and small scrub oaks and pines fell, clipped or crushed by the plummeting van. As Joe peered down the hillside a low-hanging limb smashed one of the headlights. The twin cones of light died to a single diffuse beam as useful in the darkness as a dim flashlight.

"Look!" Joe yelled, pointing. He had caught the merest glimpse of a narrow trail winding down the hillside.

"I see it," Frank said, struggling with the wheel to execute a nearly perfect turn and wind up on the trail.

The van bounced so hard that Joe felt certain his seat belt was cutting him in half. The trail hadn't been designed with cars or speed in mind. The van teetered from side to side, stones rattling against the undercarriage and pinging off the fenders.

They could now see moonlight glittering off the surface of dark water below. If Frank wasn't able to stop the van, Joe knew they would end up in the water, and there was no telling how deep it was.

"Frank," Joe yelled, watching the black water fill the entire view. "You might want to stop the van—now or never."

Frank viciously pulled the steering wheel to the right. The van heaved forward one last time before settling into the mushy terrain.

"Wow," Joe said, letting out a long, deep breath "*That* is something I'm not going to want to do again any time soon."

Frank nodded wordlessly, prying his hands from the steering wheel. He reached up and turned on the dome light, illuminating the interior of the van. "Are you okay?"

"A little banged up," Joe admitted. He looked at a red welt on his arm. "You?"

"I've been better," Frank admitted. "Lots better." He turned to look back up the hill.

Joe also turned to see the path of environmental destruction they'd left behind them, then rested his eyes straight ahead again. His gaze fell on the bullet hole in Frank's window.

Frank put his finger in the hole. "They shot at us," he said, feeling anger swell up in him.

"There were no plates on that truck, neither front nor back," Joe said. "And it appeared out of nowhere. They must have known about that curve in the road, and that that incline was one of the only ones along here. They knew *exactly* where to take us out." Quick-tempered by nature, he had no problem reaching his boiling point as he itemized and put together all the facts.

"It's no great leap of logic to figure someone was waiting for us," Frank agreed. "But why?"

"No one knew when we'd be through here exactly," Joe said.

Frank stepped on the accelerator. The engine whined as it picked up rpms. A shrill squeal came from under the hood, but it didn't sound any worse than a belt out of adjustment.

Frank shifted the transmission into low. The wheels turned, sliding in the sandy sludge and gaining no traction.

"Stuck," Joe snarled. Insects drawn by the surviving headlight buzzed against the cracked windshield.

"We've got trouble," Frank announced.

"Man, you're telling me," Joe agreed, watching the gathering insects. "Look at the size of those bugs."

"It's worse than that, Joe," Frank said slowly, his eyes focused on the rearview mirror.

Joe glanced over at his brother in irritation. "We're stuck in the sand with no one in sight, surrounded by mosquitoes that make hungry wolves look tame. We have no way of getting ourselves out and no way of getting back at the jerks who sent us here. What could be worse?"

"The jerks aren't done with us," Frank said.

Joe spun around. Long beams of headlights shone through the brush, followed by four motorcyclists hurtling down the descent.

A bullet smacked sparks against the rear of the van.

"Run!" Joe yelled, shoving against his door. It was stuck tight. When he turned to his brother, he saw that Frank's was wedged tight, too.

"Is that your alien?" Detective Reynolds asked.

Nancy peered through a door in the side of the Dumpster in the alley behind one of the Bon Homme apartment buildings. Reynolds held up a flashlight, illuminating the container's noxious contents.

There, partially covered by debris and folded over on one end, was the unmistakable green face of the alien that had killed Trey Carter.

"Somebody cut his face off," Jason blurted out from behind Nancy.

"Now that would be harsh," Tommy said somewhere farther behind Nancy.

Nancy leaned in to get a closer look at the mask the killer had used. She had to agree that the face did look as if it had been sliced right off someone's head. The light green skin ruffled over the edge of a small cardboard box beneath it.

At Nancy's side, Tarkington slipped a collapsible metal pointer out of his pocket. "Do you mind?" he asked the detective.

"Go ahead," Reynolds replied. "The crime lab guys shot a couple of preliminary pics and took some videotape footage. We still have to try to lift any prints, though."

Nancy guessed the crime lab team would have little success. The killer wouldn't have left the mask behind if it could be tied to him.

Tarkington eased the end of the pointer into the mask and opened it carefully. The interior of the mask held a powdery residue. "There are a couple of hairs in here," the FBI agent stated.

Reynolds nodded. "I've got the hairs-and-fibers team on the way."

"There could be fingerprints in the powder inside the mask," Nancy said.

Reynolds looked at the FBI agent. "You never said exactly where you got her."

A small smile touched Tarkington's lips. "You've heard of Carson Drew?"

"In this state? The kind of work I do?" Reynolds asked facetiously. "How could I not?"

"Nancy is his daughter."

Reynolds's eyes widened slightly. "Guess it's genetic."

Nancy felt a flush of pride at the reaction her father's name got and the respect given her because of it. She didn't figure she would ever get used to it.

"The fingerprints," Nancy reminded the professionals.

"The crime lab guys will go over every centimeter of it," Reynolds answered. "Don't worry, we *try* to be thorough."

Nancy ignored the veiled sarcasm. You may not like it, she said silently to him, but this is my investigation as much as yours.

She stepped back to the mouth of the short alley. Above them, a handful of people stood on fire escape landings, watching the police operation. Out on the street, a local television station van was parked against the curb. A team of three had already started setting up equipment.

Farther down the street, near the corner, two people stood inside a bus stop shelter. Both seemed to be watching the crime investigation scene. Nancy found herself walking toward them.

"Excuse me," she said when she reached the bus stop. A man in a black beret stood a distance away from an old woman wearing a plastic raincoat. They obviously weren't together.

"Are you with the police?" the man asked, making room for her to come in out of the rain.

"No," Nancy answered as she carefully studied the seat, glass, and frame of the bus stop. The heavy glass walls streamed with rain on the outside. On the inside, one of the panes also held a few small white powdery impressions. She moved in more closely, examining her find with a pen flashlight.

"Fingerprints?" Tommy asked from over her shoulder.

Startled, Nancy spoke sharply to him. "What are you doing here?"

"I got bored with the medics," Tommy said, giving her his winning smile from under the white bandage wrapped around his head. "You think those are our man's prints?"

"Yes, I do," Nancy replied. "Would you bring Agent Tarkington and Detective Reynolds over here?"

"Sure." Tommy sprinted off.

Nancy gazed across the street at the convenience store on the corner. The neon lights in the windows drew colorful, squiggly lines through the rain.

Reynolds and Tarkington appeared and Nancy pointed out the white powder smudges on the glass.

The homicide detective bellowed for a couple of the crime lab people. "Maybe we'll get lucky and this guy will be listed somewhere in the national crime computers," he growled. "We could use a bit of luck."

"Maybe we're luckier than you think," Nancy replied, gazing at the convenience store.

Tarkington followed her line of sight. "What?"

"The convenience store has a security camera," Nancy said, then pointed down the street. "So does the ATM next door. This bus stop just may be in the background of one or both of them." She was excited about the possibilities. It was one thing to get proof positive that the killer hadn't been an extraterrestrial. It was another to realize they might actually have a picture of the man.

Joe turned off the dome light just as Frank killed the remaining headlight. Darkness closed in around them as the green of the instrument panel faded from view. It wasn't much of a safeguard, but at least they wouldn't be advertising their location to their pursuers.

Joe slammed himself against his door. On the third try, the metal wrenched free. He glanced back at Frank.

"Take the cellular phone," Frank said, reaching behind the driver's seat and grabbing the notebook computer in its own waterproof backpack. Another swift grab and he held the packet of papers that had been in the compartment between the bucket seats. The men who'd set them up probably knew all about them, but it was second nature to Frank to limit the amount of information left behind.

Joe yanked the cellular phone from its mount on the dash.

"Call Eric," Frank said as he bailed out of the van after his brother. His feet sank immediately in the sandy muck surrounding the vehicle. Cold grit closed in over his shoes. With his first step, he nearly spilled over.

The racing motorcyclists were getting closer.

"Eric and his buddies can probably get here faster than the state police," Frank said. "But call nine one one after you get off the phone with him."

Bullets suddenly pocked huge holes in the muck around them.

Chapter

Four

THEY'RE NOT SHOOTING to hit us," Joe surmised.

"Maybe," Frank admitted. "Or maybe they're just lousy shots."

"They may have an advantage now, on those bikes," Joe growled, "but the first one of them I get my hands on is going to realize the mistake he's made."

"Joe, just stay out of their reach," Frank advised. His gaze raked the wooded incline behind them and the black water spread out before them. No obvious means of escape showed itself. Frank's mind raced. Who would be after them and why? Unless their pursuers had them confused with someone else. He and Joe weren't working on anything—they were supposed to be on vacation.

He peered around the corner of the van. The motorcyclists had divided into two sets of two and had picked up the pace.

"If we split up, we've got a better chance of avoiding them." Frank said. "I've got the phone and modem on the computer. You keep the cellular."

Joe nodded. "Agreed." He waved toward the water. "Wet and wild, or flora and fauna?" He pointed toward the scrubby trees.

The motorcycle roars were almost on top of them.

"Wet and wild," Frank said.

"Okay," Joe agreed. "See you." He moved toward the front of the van and the pines.

"Be careful," Frank warned Joe. He looked at the dark water and tried not to think about what might be in there.

"Think dry thoughts," Joe offered. Then he melted into the shadows, leaving behind only the sound of his running steps. Twenty feet into the trees, a headlight lanced the darkness and caught him for just a moment, freezing him in full stride. Then he was gone.

Frank took three steps out into the pond water. It rose to his chest, then the bottom dropped out from under him and the cold black water closed over his head. The backpack was waterproof, so he didn't think twice about the computer.

He surfaced easily and swam in short, powerful strokes. A glance over his shoulder showed him that two of the motorcycles were pursuing Joe.

The other two came to a halt near the van, their headlights playing over the water.

"There," a man shouted in accented English.

Frank watched his shadow suddenly materialize around him as the light from the motorcycles fell across him. He took a deep breath and dove beneath the water.

The scaled flesh of a snake glided across his cheek as quick as hot oil and as cool as ice. Then he felt strong coils wrap around his left arm.

Frank broke the surface of the water, trying to escape the hold. He lifted his left arm and shook it vigorously, but the snake's cold coils only tightened. Frank could feel his heartbeat throbbing in the veins of his arm.

Off balance and too stunned to tread water skillfully, Frank made more noise than he'd intended. As he sank below the surface, he heard a man yell, "Over there! In the water!"

Frank continued to flail underwater, trying to shake off the snake. At least three feet in length, it held fast within easy striking distance. Its head glided through the water toward Frank's face. Illuminated by the powerful motorcycle lights on shore, everything took on a slow-motion, surreal quality as the snake lunged.

Frank yelled reflexively, spewing bubbles of precious oxygen out of his mouth and obscuring his view of the snake. He reached out blindly toward his eely enemy, the water slowing his usually quick, precise movements. His hand closed around the snake's body just behind the head. Colubrid, he told himself, identifying his foe. Colubridae are nonvenomous. In Frank's stranglehold, the snake finally uncoiled itself.

Frank kicked to the surface, gasping as he broke through to the night air. He held the snake underwater.

"I've lost him," one of the men yelled.

The words carried over the water, but barely reached Frank's ears over the amplified sound of his own heavy breathing.

Frank drew his arm up and threw the snake as far as he could. Its rubbery body arced through the air before slamming back into the water.

The lights from the shore instantly tracked the sound, then followed the motion of the snake swimming through the water to shore.

Frank drew in a deep breath and swam for a bank twenty feet in the other direction.

Searchlights panned the water's surface in smaller and smaller circles. As Frank's foot touched sandy bottom, the light shone in a circle around him. "Halt!" a man ordered.

Fat chance, Frank thought. He crouched low, trying to obtain some cover.

"Halt or we'll shoot!"

Ignoring the command, Frank raced up on to the bank and headed for the pines twenty feet away. Motorcycle engines thrummed in the distance, rising and falling on the air. That meant that Joe was still free and running.

Bullets suddenly slapped the sand around

Frank. He dove forward and landed on soft sandy soil behind the trunk of a fallen tree.

He crawled on his belly until he reached the protection of more trees. Finally feeling safe, he glanced back and spotted the motorcyclists working their way toward him. Besides being very well equipped and informed, the men chasing Joe and him showed a lot of determination.

He just wished he knew what was going on.

"You're going to have to tweak the resolution more," Tommy Buskirk advised. He was referring to the almost indecipherable videotape appropriated by Detective Reynolds from the convenience store across from the bus stop.

The police computer specialist shot Tommy a look of annoyance. "Look, kid, I've been doing this a long time."

"I can tell," Tommy replied with earnest intent. "The CAD program you're using has got to be at least six months old. And that motherboard, man." He shook his head in disbelief. "Have you ever heard of MMX technology?"

Across the room, Nancy Drew hid her smile behind a cup of hot chocolate she had gotten from the snack room in the police station. When Tommy got into his area of expertise, he could be difficult. Invaluable, but difficult.

The paunchy computer cop groaned. "Kid, you're getting on my last nerve here." He looked up at Reynolds. "Arnie, do I have to put up with this?"

"No." Reynolds covered the mouthpiece of the phone he held. "As soon as you get that picture blown up so we can ID the perp, I'll make him stop and go away. Promise."

Reynolds held up a hand to silence any further complaints and returned to his phone call. He was, after all, on a conference call with technicians at all three area crime labs getting an update on any evidence that would pinpoint Carter's murderer.

"Tommy's right," Special Agent Tarkington said to Nancy. "The video-enhancement system here is the equivalent of trying to run uphill with only one lung working. The techs at Quantico would have already printed out the finished product."

"Everybody's a critic," the police computer man said. "Ol' Bessie here hasn't ever let me down." He patted the computer monitor affectionately.

Nancy took another sip of her hot chocolate. The liquid had cooled enough to go down easily. It was her second cup of the hot, sugary brew, but the residual chill from her wet clothes still ate bone deep.

"Another six months and Ol' Bessie won't even qualify as an organ donor in the field of cybernetics," Tommy promised.

The police officer made a rude noise and turned his attention back to the keyboard.

Nancy walked over to have a look. The image on the screen was frozen at the moment that

Carter's killer had stripped off his alien mask. The picture appeared to be too grainy to blow up properly and reveal the man's features, but they all had hopes.

Nancy's eyes felt grainy as well, and she knew they were probably bloodshot. After she had suggested that the killer might have been video-taped, it had taken almost an hour to get a court order for the convenience store's tapes. The clock on the wall over Reynolds's head now read 3:25 A.M. in bright red LCD numbers.

"You did good out there tonight," Tarkington said out of the blue.

"Thank you," Nancy answered with honest surprise. Since they had arrived back at the police station, the FBI agent had been almost silent. Nancy's intuition told her there was more on Tarkington's mind than simply turning the case over to the local PD. She wanted to snoop around the agent's thoughts, but she couldn't think of a way to get the stony man talking.

The picture on the computer monitor rippled again as colors sparkled across the screen. Then more of the fog lifted, and the features on the killer's face came into sharper focus.

Nancy heard Tarkington's sharp intake of breath and guessed the agent had just been surprised.

On the computer screen, the man's face was revealed amidst shadows cast from a scraggly tree. He had been caught in the process of yanking his mask up and off his head. His forehead was still green, the rest of his face was pale gray. The lack of clear detail made it look as if he were actually pulling his own face off.

The man's features were blunt and the shape of his face vaguely triangular. His eyes were spaced far apart and slitted. A faded scar rippled along his left cheek, from his cheekbone to the point of his chin. It wasn't a face that could easily be forgotten.

"You know him, don't you?" Nancy asked Tarkington.

Everyone in the room turned toward the FBI agent—even Jason, who was at another desk on the phone with the owner of the radio station.

"Yes, I know him," Tarkington said with a sigh of resignation. "That's Amos Jericho. And I have to admit he's looking pretty good for a man who was killed three years ago."

Joe's lungs burned as he ran, but the sound of the motorcycles seemed farther behind him. At the ridge, he peered back toward the water where he'd left Frank. He had heard gunshots while he was running, but there had been no time to stop to see what had happened to his brother.

Even if the shots didn't mean Frank was wounded—or worse—Joe's imagination filled the water with all kinds of dangerous creatures, stopping just short of a velociraptor. I should have taken the water, Joe chided himself. Then he made himself stop: negative thinking doesn't help, Hardy.

Joe pushed off again and drove his legs hard. Luckily, baseball season wasn't that long over, and he'd been staying in shape for the upcoming football season.

Spotting another rise, he angled up toward it. The ocean wasn't far off; the smell of salt was thick in the air.

He reached a large oak tree at the top of the rise in seconds and stooped down into the grasses that surrounded it. Peering back the way he'd come, he saw the van mired in the sandy muck. And three motorcycle headlights.

The two that were farthest away assured Joe that Frank was still running free. He smiled at that, feeling some of the tension unwind from his chest. No matter how prepared their attackers were, they couldn't have known how good the Hardy brothers were at dodging thugs—even when caught off guard.

The third motorcycle was about seventy yards away and showed no sign of moving any closer, but where was the fourth? Joe hoped it had gotten bogged down or wrapped around a tree or . . .

Joe shook the fantasies out of his head and snapped open the cellular phone. He was pretty sure, with Wedge Grove so close, a phone tower would pick up the signal.

Joe punched in Eric's number at the institute. Eric had said he'd wait there for them until they arrived. Joe hoped no one had seen the eerie glow of the key pad.

"Wedge Grove Oceanography Institute," a female voice answered.

Joe was startled because he knew the institute was closed and had expected Eric to answer. "Who am I speaking to?" he asked.

"Mandy MacMahon," she replied with a no-nonsense edge to her voice. "Who am *I* talking to?"

"Joe Hardy."

"Oh." Mandy's voice relaxed. "Eric's friend."

"Not his only one, I hope," Joe quipped. From the silence on the other end of the line, he knew his joke hadn't scored. The sound of racing motorcycle engines drew his attention back to his current situation.

"What can I do for you, Joe?" she asked.

"Is Eric around?" Joe didn't want to drop his news on her. Eric would take him seriously, and he'd act immediately, but it would take time to convince this woman.

"I think he's in the mess."

A crackle of static rippled across the connection, blurring some of her words. "That sounds like Eric," Joe said. "He's always in a mess. What is it this time?"

"Not *a* mess," Mandy said impatiently. "*The* mess. The galley. The kitchen. He's getting a snack."

"Got you. Would it be a problem to talk to him?" If it was, he'd have to call 911 instead.

"No." Mandy yelled Eric's name loudly, obviously without covering the mouthpiece of her phone.

Joe winced and pulled the cellular phone away from his ear.

"Where are you?" Mandy asked, returning to the phone. "I thought Eric said you and your brother would be here by now."

"We'd planned to be," Joe replied. "We sort of got waylaid."

"Nothing serious, I hope."

"An inconvenience," Joe lied. Later, when Mandy found out what the brothers had been through, he could imagine how impressed she'd be.

"Here's Eric."

"Thanks," Joe said.

"Yo, Twitch," Eric said in his booming, jovial voice. "You're late. I'd have expected that of you if you were by yourself, but I felt relatively safe with Frank along."

"Right," Joe replied, his tone serious. "We'll all chuckle later, okay? Right now, Frank and I have a problem." He quickly relayed the situation.

"Say no more, Twitch. Can you tell me where?"

"I can get you close." Joe sketched out the approximate location of the hill where they'd been forced off the road.

"I know the place," Eric said. "Give me your cell phone number. As soon as I get moving, I'll call. Stay loose, Twitch," Eric advised. "The cavalry's on the way."

"Be careful," Joe said, scanning the trees again. He disconnected the phone and felt as if he were letting go of a lifeline. Then he began to dial 911.

Before he got to the second digit, however, cold metal touched his cheek. He instantly recognized the cool smoothness of the business end of a very big pistol.

Chapter

Five

"NO FAST MOVES and I don't empty your brain pan," said the man with the gun.

Joe stared down the length of the automatic pistol. His voice felt tight when he spoke, "Sure. No sudden moves." Loosening up his vocal cords, he added, "Is your aim as good as your English?"

"Don't make me mad," the man said flatly. "Give me the phone."

"They're probably both better than your sense of humor," Joe replied as he passed the cellular phone across. He had taken a big chance, but it worked. The armed giant had watched Joe's face as he was mouthing off and missed the slight movement of Joe's finger twice pressing the number one button to finish his 911 call.

"What's this about?" Joe asked, trying to buy

time and cover the sound of the phone ringing on the other end of the line. Maybe, he hoped, he could get a word to 911.

"Shut your mouth," the man instructed. "Or die."

"Sure. Whatever you say."

The man reached forward and tapped Joe's forehead with the pistol muzzle hard enough to bring a brief burst of pain.

"Nine-one-one operator," a male voice said over the cellular phone. "Please state the nature of your emergency and your location."

The gunman lowered the pistol to rest on Joe's lips as he punched the phone off and dropped it in a pocket of his coveralls. "Hands behind your back."

Joe clasped his hands behind his back, interlacing his fingers, saying nothing.

The gunman put a pair of plastic Saf-T-Kufs on Joe's wrists and cinched them tight. "Now stand up and move forward," the man ordered.

Joe started walking. After a few steps, he heard the electronic warble of a walkie-talkie behind him.

His captor spoke briefly in a language that sounded Slavic, but Joe was only halfway sure. The situation was definitely getting weirder. Who were these guys, and what did they want with him and Frank?

Frank opened the backpack while deep in a stand of brush. Then he wiped his hands on the grass before opening the notebook computer inside.

A few minutes ago the sound of the motorcycles had died away, along with their lights, and Frank had lost track of where his pursuers were. He had been relying on the noise of the racing engines as evidence that Joe was still up and running. He didn't like thinking what the silence could mean.

Frank lifted the cellular phone from the computer pack. They kept one with the portable computer so while they were linked up with the Internet service they used, they'd have the other cellular free.

Frank punched 911 on the keypad. He wanted the operator he reached to tell him they were already responding to Joe's call.

A branch breaking to his left and behind him warned him of the danger too late. He froze, the phone receiver to his ear.

A bright flashlight suddenly flared in his eyes.

"Put the phone down or die!" a rough voice said.

Frank tried to stare past the light but couldn't. He heard the phone ring a second time.

Suddenly a pistol flared in front of him, and the sound of the shot deafened him. Then rough hands seized him from behind, clamping him in place and yanking the phone from his hand.

"Face down!" another voice ordered.

Frank was pushed forward on the rough ground. A rock grazed his cheek. Someone punched the cellular phone off, then took the computer backpack away. Someone else pulled his hands behind his back and cuffed him.

"Get up," the man with the pistol commanded.

"What's this about?" Frank asked as he struggled to his feet unaided. He peered through the darkness, noting how the man was covered in camouflage cosmetics and wearing coveralls.

"We ask the questions," the man replied. "You answer."

"What about my brother?"

"He's alive."

Frank breathed a sigh of relief. Joe so often let his temper get the better of him—even in the face of overwhelming odds like these—that Frank was sure he'd just go and get his head blown off someday.

"If you are a lucky man," his armed captor said, almost growling, "you, too, will continue to be alive."

That, Frank decided, didn't sound promising.

"Dead?" Jason Watson croaked, turning around at the desk he'd borrowed to make his calls. "That guy was not dead!"

"I'm not saying that guy was dead, but we heard Jericho was dead." The FBI agent appeared slightly uncomfortable, but Nancy had to give him credit. He was recovering well.

"We only thought there was a possibility Carter wasn't working alone in the scam for the tickets for the *Titanic* cruise," Tarkington admitted.

Ol' Bessie's ancient printer laboriously ejected a color copy of Jericho's image, then subsided into silence. Reynolds retrieved the printout and flicked the paper with a forefinger. The pop of the paper sounded loud in the small room. *"We?"* he asked. "This is getting more interesting all the time."

"You said your office didn't know anything about the ticket giveaway scam until my father contacted you on behalf of WUUL," Nancy challenged the agent.

"That was true, but in our preliminary exploration of this investigation, we turned up Amos Jericho's name."

"Maybe you should start there," Nancy suggested. "Who is Jericho and how do you know him?"

"And remember, pal," Reynolds added, "I'll be checking up on what you say."

Tarkington crossed the room to the office coffee pot and helped himself to another cup. He turned to face the group. "Amos Jericho is a national embarrassment. Potentially he could create an international incident. And he's not working alone."

Jason had gotten up from his desk and stood next to Nancy. "You knew all this before we went there tonight?" he charged.

"No," Tarkington replied evenly. "As I said, we knew that it was *possible* Trey Carter was working with Jericho."

"Would Carter know who he was working for?" Nancy asked.

"Probably not. Jericho would have worked under an alias. When you came to us about the ticket scam, we were already investigating the *Titanic* cruise. It's no secret that a great number of people feel Walter Welsch should leave the shipwreck alone."

Nancy knew that was true. For weeks the national news had been full of reports of demonstrations against Welsch's raising even a portion of the wrecked vessel. Some of the demonstrations had almost become violent.

"One of our agents out in California working on a private art gallery robbery thought that maybe Jericho had a hand in it."

"The Costanza family's gallery?" Nancy asked. "What's the connection with you?" She was familiar with the robbery because a friend of her father's in San Luis Obispo had called him for advice on cracking it. When the story broke in the news, there had been no mention of FBI interest.

Surprise flickered through the FBI agent's eyes. "I'm not at liberty to say."

"Okay, so you got this lead from California. I don't see the tie here." Reynolds seemed to be on the offensive.

"All right, everyone just calm down," Tarkington ordered. "If you asked for the FBI file, it would tell you that Jericho was CIA, primarily in Eastern Europe, in the eighties. He worked deep cover a lot, using at least a dozen different names. Even the Central Intelligence Agency couldn't keep up with everything he had going.

"When the Berlin Wall fell in 1989, Jericho instantly became a dinosaur. There was little need for spies any longer. A swift, quiet retirement was all he had in his future. He turned rogue, an independent spy for hire to the highest bidder, and went into business with some of the Communists he'd been spying on. He specialized in helping deposed Communist leaders get their wealth out of their countries."

"Jericho worked alone?" Nancy asked.

"No, it wasn't just Jericho. He put together a team of men and women to help him. He gathered them from both sides of the Iron Curtain. People who'd once been enemies were now allies."

"It wasn't about politics anymore," Tommy said.

Tarkington nodded his head in agreement. "It was about money. Lots of it. Millions were secretly taken out of the emerging democracies over there. Amos Jericho and his team of specialists were the best of their kind."

"That doesn't explain why Jericho would be interested in tickets for the *Titanic* cruise," Jason pointed out.

"Think about it," Tarkington encouraged.

"Walter Welsch is planning to raise a section of the *Titanic* a few days from now, along with whatever's still on board—"

"You think Jericho and Welsch could be in on this together?" Reynolds asked excitedly. "You think they're going to try to steal whatever artifacts they raise and sell them on the black market?"

"That's just one of many reasons why Welsch shouldn't be allowed to raise the *Titanic,*" Tommy burst out.

"I know your moral standards are as high for yourself as for others—" Nancy began sympathetically.

"I don't want to argue the morality of raising the *Titanic* right now," Tommy interrupted her. "Let's just say I don't agree with Welsch's idea of raising the ship."

"That's okay, buddy," a new voice said from behind Nancy, "I'm not going to hold your opinion against you."

"The guys on motorcycles had night vision glasses," Joe whispered to Frank. They were sitting beside their van while two men kept watch on them with drawn guns. "No wonder we couldn't hide from them. With the glasses, they were picking up our body heat even in the shadows. We never had a chance."

Frank, too, had noted the NVGs around the necks of their captors. The thick-bodied headsets tapering out to monocular tubes were unmistakable.

Three men were going through their van with flashlights. Most of Frank and Joe's belongings were scattered in the sand, and some had wound up in the pond.

Their two captors conferred quickly. Frank thought he recognized the language as a Russian derivative but couldn't be sure.

A third man, who had been standing in the shadows, appeared to be the leader as he came forward and snapped his fingers with obvious irritation. Frank and Joe's two guards quickly patted them down, stripping them of their wallets.

Using a pen flashlight, the leader went through the wallets carefully. He made a show of comparing the pictures on the driver's licenses to his captives.

"You are Frank and Joe Hardy," he stated, putting the boys' wallets in a pocket of his coverall.

"Yes," Frank answered. What else was there to say? Especially since they must have already known that.

"What are you doing here?"

"We're on a trip," Frank said.

"Where are you going?" the man asked.

"To Oz." Joe snorted his anger in biting sarcasm. "Or didn't you notice the Yellow Brick Road?"

The leader glanced at the man standing beside Joe. The captor stepped forward and rapped his pistol against Joe's skull.

Joe yelped in pain, then, because his wrists were still cuffed, he tried to butt his attacker with his head. Another man joined the first and they slammed Joe back to the ground. All Frank could do was shake his head.

"I ask *you*," the leader said to Frank, "where were you going?"

"Wedge Grove Oceanography Institute," Frank answered.

"Why?"

"To see a friend."

"What friend?"

"Eric Cox." Frank studied the man's face, trying to read if Eric's name meant anything to him. Apparently not.

"Why were you going to see him?"

"We were invited."

The leader lifted his chin slightly, his eyes narrowing. "If I must continue having to drag answers from you, I'll have your brother shot. Don't worry. I won't have him killed, just crippled."

"It's a personal visit," Frank replied. It wasn't worth taking a chance on whether or not the man was bluffing. "Eric Cox is a friend from school who's working at the institute for the summer. He invited us up for a week of sailing and snorkeling. That's all."

The leader paused before he asked his next question. "Your father is Fenton Hardy."

Frank nodded. His father's reputation was international, and it wasn't a stretch to believe his captors had heard of him.

"That's right," Joe piped up. "And you can bet that if anything happens to us, he's not going to stop turning over rocks until he finds the slugs who are responsible."

The leader fortunately ignored Joe's outburst. "Your father did not send you here?" he asked Frank.

"No."

The leader glanced from Frank to Joe, then back again. Finally he turned to the men searching the van. "Did you find anything?"

One of them stepped outside the vehicle and snapped his flashlight off in disgust. "Nothing."

Frank wondered what they were looking for, but he came up short. All of their captors were professionals, and he and Joe had been taken— alive—with an economy of effort.

He tried to remember everything Eric had told him about the institute. Could these men have anything to do with Wedge Grove, or could they have something against it? Nothing came to mind.

"Perhaps you should enjoy a piece of advice," the leader said, turning back to Frank.

Frank remained silent. Advice meant a future. That looked pretty good at the moment.

"Cut your visit short," the man said, tossing their wallets to the ground. "Go back to Bayport and tell your father to forget any of this ever happened."

"Maybe you'd better start running," Joe growled. *"I'm* not going to forget this happened."

"Then you are a fool," the leader said coldly, "and you'll soon be a dead fool—the next time I see or even smell you."

For a second Frank thought the hammering in the air was the sound of distant thunder. Then it neared and he realized it came from an approaching helicopter.

The gunmen all looked skyward.

Frank did the same, spotting the searchlight that flared down from the front of the white helicopter. Dark letters on the side announced Wedge Grove Oceanography Institute.

The gunmen scattered and took off up the hill and into the trees, three of them pulling Frank and Joe along with them.

"Shoot it down!" the leader ordered from off to the left. He leveled his pistol and prepared to fire.

Frank gazed at the helicopter, which was no more than thirty feet above the tallest trees. He realized then that Joe must have gotten through to Eric, who got a team to come looking for them.

Fear chilled Frank's blood even more than the gritty muck that covered him as he watched the aircraft close in. When it got into firing range, it would be as good as a sitting duck.

Frank glanced over at Joe as the Wedge Grove helicopter drew closer. No way could they allow Eric and his friends to be shot down. He saw his own grim determination reflected in his brother's eyes. They went into action together.

Frank threw himself to the right, colliding with a gunman hard enough to knock him into another man. Both fell to the ground. The man's pistol discharged into the ground. The sudden blast of sound ricocheted through the trees.

Frank hoped the people in the helicopter had heard the shot or at least noticed the muzzle flash. He rolled back on his shoulders, throwing his hands as far down as he could reach, and barely managed to get his manacled hands under his feet and up in front of him. He stood up, taking cover behind a tree.

Frank saw Joe running toward a gunman drawing a rifle bead on the approaching aircraft.

Horror raced through Frank when the gunman whirled on his brother.

Chapter

Six

NANCY TURNED. She recognized the tall, lean man at once. Walter Welsch, at one time or another, had graced the cover of every national magazine.

Welsch wore an expensive-looking Italian suit the color of old rust. Nancy would have bet it had been tailor made. His boots—not shoes—had to be Italian as well, dark leather with fancy stitching. His dark, close-cropped hair and mocking, wry smile had been made familiar by the media. In his early thirties, single, wealthy, and tanned, he was one of the world's most eligible bachelors.

"Sorry to be so late," he said. "Some parties you just seem never to be able to leave."

Reynolds fixed the billionaire with a hard glare. "Why are you here?"

"The shooting made the news," Welsch explained. "I watch the news a lot—sometimes all night. I got interested and came here to see what you people were doing. After all, the media is getting a lot of mileage out of my name and the *Titanic* cruise." He crossed the room and sat on the corner of the desk Jason had vacated. "Hello—Jason Watson? Is that right?"

"Hello, Mr. Welsch," Jason answered after nodding.

With that simple address, Nancy watched Jason become the boy she remembered from high school. Jason was evidently very impressed with the billionaire.

"Anyway," Welsch went on, "I decided it might be in my best interests to find out what was going on. I called my lawyer, who made a couple of calls to some people here at the police department." He fingered the ID badge clipped to his jacket pocket. "It doesn't exactly go with the suit, but I found it helped get me through the building."

"Mr. Welsch," Reynolds said, "you really shouldn't be here."

Welsch smiled warmly, lacing his fingers together. "That's not how my attorney feels. He thinks I have a right to show interest in how this investigation proceeds because it may reflect on a project in which I have invested heavily. I tend to agree."

The phone on Reynolds's desk rang. He spoke briefly, gazing at Welsch during the whole conversation. At least, it looked like a conversation. The detective said yes twice, then hung up. He seemed pretty unhappy as he turned to Tarkington. "Why don't you finish filling me—and Mr. Welsch—in on Jericho. He's been cleared." Reynolds jerked his head in Welsch's direction.

An uncomfortable silence settled over the group. Nancy made a mental bet with herself as to who was going to break the silence. She won.

"Who or what is this Jericho and how is he connected to my *Titanic* operation," Mr. Welsch asked the FBI man.

"You also said he'd been dead for three years," Nancy pointed out. "Why?"

"That's what the paperwork here shows," Reynolds said. In the short while since Tarkington had identified the killer, he had faxed Washington and received a response. "A report filed by Britain's MI-6, its intelligence-gathering group, three years ago states that Amos Jericho, Carter's killer, died in a warehouse fire in London."

"After tonight," Tarkington said, "we know that couldn't be true. The report stated that Jericho had arranged to sell weapons to the Irish Republican Army. The operation was uncovered and the sale quashed. His body was never found, but there was solid evidence pointing to his death from an explosion or fire at the warehouse where the arms were stored."

"Given that this man is still alive," Welsch said, "what would his interest be in the *Titanic?*"

"In the years since the Wall fell," Tarkington

said, "Amos Jericho has been involved in art robberies—big-time art robberies—in addition to his other illegal activities. He was privy to a lot of useful information during his career in the CIA."

"He knows where the bodies are buried," Reynolds stated.

"Exactly. And he knows which collectors are vulnerable. There are a number of them around the globe whose holdings are not listed with insurance companies."

"Collectors don't always bother with the legalities of ownership," Tommy stated. "You find a lot of computer hackers who have the same principles regarding software."

Tarkington nodded. "One of Jericho's main interests while he was in Eastern Europe was art."

"And certain kinds of art are easily transportable and don't lose their value," Nancy said. She saw where the FBI agent was going with his conversation.

Tarkington nodded. "Jericho favored—excuse me, favors—gems and jewelry for the same reasons."

"You think Amos Jericho linked up with Trey Carter to get the tickets for the cruise?" Jason said. "It seems silly for a guy with so much money to steal two-thousand-dollar tickets. Why not buy one—or ten, even?"

The FBI agent shrugged. "Maybe he enjoys the act of stealing. I don't know."

Welsch grinned. "This is fascinating. You actually think this Jericho is after whatever valuables we might turn up when we raise the *Titanic?*"

Nancy felt that at the very least, the mystery was getting more interesting. She still couldn't understand why Jericho would kill Carter, though. Nancy had been lost in her thoughts and was startled to realize that Welsch was still speaking.

"Do you realize how many people are going to be out there on the ocean when we bring up the *Titanic?*" Welsch asked. "There's no way Jericho could get away with stealing things."

"Remember, Mr. Welsch," Tarkington said, "there was no way the *Titanic* could sink, either. The list I could give you concerning the thefts Jericho and his group have performed would stagger you. I think you'd be a believer if you saw it."

"Agent Tarkington is right," Reynolds announced, sliding the sheaf of papers he'd accumulated from the printer over to Welsch. "Since you'll probably be able to get a copy of this yourself, go ahead and take a look."

Calmly and coolly, Welsch crossed the room and took the papers.

Curious, Nancy walked over to the billionaire. "May I?"

Welsch flipped through the pages, handing them off to her. "You're Ms. Drew, aren't you?"

"Yes," Nancy answered. She took the pages. Just glancing at the geography involved in Amos

Jericho's career was astounding. The man traveled the globe.

"Jason has told me about you," Welsch said. "It's enchanting to meet you."

Nancy's face flushed. "Thank you. How do you know Jason?"

"His employer and I are friends, and I met Jason through him. His employer told me about the night's activities."

Nancy tried to concentrate on the file she was going through, but she found it was almost impossible. She'd been around rich and powerful men before, but Welsch exuded an aura that was almost physical.

"All right then," Welsch stated, handing the last of the papers to Nancy and turning his attention back to Tarkington and Reynolds. "You've convinced me of the possibility that this man could be dangerous to my work—regardless of the crack security staff that will be on hand for the raising. What would you suggest?"

"For starters," Reynolds said, "I'd cancel the cruise."

Welsch shook his head. "I'm not willing to do that. I always stand by my agreements and contracts. I made an agreement with each ticket purchaser that he or she would be part of a historic moment. I won't go back on that."

"Then, a good beginning would be to check out all the winners of the WUUL tickets," Nancy interjected.

"That's a good suggestion. Thank you,

Nancy." Welsch favored her with a hundred-watt smile. He turned back to Tarkington. "I've already noticed on the ship's roster that some of the passengers aboard the *Hampton* are people with ties to the FBI."

Tarkington didn't bother to deny the allegation.

"I assume you'll put those people on alert to search for Jericho and his band of thieves."

Tarkington nodded.

Nancy wasn't surprised that the FBI would go along on the trip. A number of influential people had gone down with the *Titanic,* and over the decades since, there had been speculation regarding what might be recovered in the ship's safes. Some of the documents and papers aboard would be better left undiscovered, or so the tabloids had screamed over the last few weeks.

What effect would a time capsule from 1912 have on current world politics and business? Nancy thought as Welsch posed another question.

"If, for the last three years Amos Jericho has been believed dead, then where was he?"

"I'd like to know the answer to that one myself," Reynolds said, glancing at Tarkington.

"We're not sure," the FBI agent replied. "When our agents in California were looking into the Costanza gallery robbery, they thought it could have been done by Jericho. Then they got a lead that suggested the warehouse fire hadn't killed Jericho but had seriously harmed him. With the money he'd made, he would have enough to afford a prolonged convalescence."

"Judging from the way he was moving," Nancy said, "there's nothing wrong with him now."

"I'll have to operate on that assumption," Welsch said. "I'll alert my staff. Maybe with all of us working on it we can trap Jericho and his people if they decide to continue with this venture." He flicked his eyes back to Nancy. "It seems I owe you a debt of gratitude, Ms. Drew."

"No," Nancy replied. "I was just helping Jason."

Welsch inclined his head in a courtly gesture that Nancy found flattering. "And, in turn, you succeeded in making me aware of this potential problem. Raising the *Titanic* means a lot to me, the fulfillment of a childhood dream, actually. I wouldn't want anything to diminish that. So I would like to offer you something to express my gratitude: a ticket for the *Titanic* cruise." He raised an eyebrow. "If you'll allow me the indulgence of asking at such late notice."

Before Nancy could reply, Tommy stepped forward. "No way, Nancy. If Amos Jericho gets onto that ship and finds out you're there and nearly helped catch him, he might kill you!"

"Please," Welsch said indignantly. "Give me more credit than that. The security staff I've employed for the *Hampton* is one of the best—"

"Yeah," Tommy said, stepping closer to the billionaire. "That's what you say. But it's Nancy's life you're gambling with."

Welsch remained calm in the face of Tommy's emotional outburst. He turned to Nancy. "Ms. Drew, ultimately the decision is yours. However, I'd like to encourage you to take the trip. You may bring friends if you'd like. Mr. Buskirk, for one, might be interested in coming along to make sure you're properly cared for."

Nancy spoke calmly. "The chances of Amos Jericho being on the *Hampton* after tonight have got to be remote."

"Or, with Trey Carter dead," Tommy argued, "Jericho may figure the coast is clear. He doesn't know we've got pictures of him stripping off his mask."

"Jericho has always operated intelligently," Tarkington said. "That's why the man has never been caught. The odds are that he won't show."

"Why take the chance?" Tommy demanded.

Welsch smiled. "Agreed. Why take the chance on missing the opportunity of a lifetime? To be one of the few who see part of the *Titanic* returned to the surface?" He paused. "Well, Ms. Drew, will you come?"

Joe watched the rifle being leveled at him. The gunman reacted more quickly than Joe had thought possible. But there was no time for regrets. He couldn't have watched Eric's being blasted from the sky without doing anything about it.

In an all-out effort, he threw himself forward in a flying block, hoping the gunman's bullets would miss him. He heard the rifle chatter in his ears and waited for the agony of bullets tearing into his flesh.

Instead, he smashed into the gunman's legs and knocked him to the ground. Joe went down in a rolling heap with the man. Landing awkwardly, Joe's breath whooshed from his lungs.

"Joe!"

He couldn't draw in a breath to yell back to Frank that he was all right. He flailed weakly trying to get to his feet while the downed gunman easily sprinted away.

The guy's got to be a pro, Joe thought as the man disappeared. That was my best shot.

He struggled to get to his feet again. Then he stretched his arms down and stepped back between them so he'd have his bound hands in front of him. The beating rotors of the helicopter overhead created a downdraft that whipped grit and debris into his face. He raised his arms to protect his head, when suddenly he heard automatic weapons roaring from the helicopter. Peering up over his arm, he spotted muzzle flashes coming from a figure standing on the landing skids of the helicopter.

"Joe!" Frank rushed to his brother's side.

"Wow," Joe said. "Eric must have brought a

platoon of marines with him." He gave his brother a crooked grin. "I'm okay." He held up his hands. "Look. No holes."

"That was stupid," Frank said. "You could have been killed."

"You and me both," Joe responded.

Frank smiled wryly. "Okay, you and me both—stupid, but alive."

"Where did they go?" Joe asked, checking around for their gun-toting friends.

"They took off."

"Cowards," Joe declared.

The searchlight located them and held them in a circle of white light.

"They may have run off, but they're not necessarily gone!" Frank yelled to Joe, realizing that the light made them perfect targets for their ex-captors.

Chapter

Seven

FRANK AND JOE WAVED the aircraft off and took cover.

"What's wrong with those guys?" Joe yelled over the whirling rotors. "They should be taking off after the gunmen." In the distance, he heard the sound of motorcycle and truck engines start up and then quickly fade. "Too late."

"That helicopter's not exactly an attack vehicle," Frank said. "Maybe they're choosing discretion."

A ladder spilled out of the Wedge Grove helicopter and hung down in a small clearing. A man's voice blared over a PA system. "Frank and Joe Hardy!"

"If I didn't know better," Frank said, "I'd swear that was one of the Gray Man's agents."

Joe knew exactly what his brother was talking

about. The words were firm and clipped, brooking no nonsense. The Gray Man was a top official of the Network, one of the United States' ultrasecret spying agencies. Every Network operative they'd encountered had been cut from the same cloth.

"Hey," Eric Cox's voice came over the PA system, "are you guys all right?"

The brothers simultaneously raised their cuffed hands, giving Eric the thumbs-up sign.

A rope spun out of the aircraft's door, and before its end had even touched ground, a man was rappelling down it.

"Look at him go," Frank said appreciatively as the guy slid down the sixty feet of rope in a couple of heartbeats.

Despite his speed, the man touched down lightly. He wore matching dark blue shirt and pants, and a dark blue baseball cap. Patches with Wedge Grove Oceanography Institute in gold lettering were on his shirt and hat. He carried an M-16 easily in his right hand.

"Norman Lowell," he said, curtly identifying himself. He slipped a lock-back knife out from his belt and flicked open the blade. "Chief of security."

Joe felt the urge to salute the man.

"Good to see you, Mr. Lowell," Frank greeted. He held his hands out and Lowell slipped the knife across the Saf-T-Kufs. The plastic parted instantly.

"You should be going after those guys," Joe said.

Lowell's lean face and light-colored eyes swept over Joe. "Those guys had guns," he explained in a quiet, controlled voice. "I was willing to commandeer a vehicle for a rescue mission, but I'm not willing to explain loss or damage of said vehicle on a civilian manhunt to the people who cut my check."

"They're going to get away," Joe protested as Lowell sliced off his cuffs, too.

"Only if they can outrun the state police," Lowell replied with a thin grin.

"They've been notified?" Frank asked.

Lowell gave him a tight nod. "First thing. Care to join us aboard the helicopter?"

Frank took the lead, swarming up the dangling ladder with ease. Joe went next, and Lowell, slipping his M-16 over his shoulder, brought up the rear.

As he stepped into the helicopter, Joe looked back down to the ground. This isn't over, yet, he thought.

Lowell agreed to let the helicopter pilot take a spin around the area on the off chance that they might see the men who had attacked Frank and Joe.

"You'd think there would be something," Eric Cox said. All spoken communication took place through the radio headsets each passenger wore.

Frank nodded, lowering the binoculars Eric had lent him. "We may have to come back in the morning."

"By then it'll be too late." Eric's rich ebony skin took on a velvety tone in the moonlight that filtered through the Plexiglas windows. Cut-off jeans and a superhero T-shirt stretched across his tall, broad frame. "You don't know who those guys were?"

"No," Frank said. "But they were waiting for us. They knew our van and they knew about when we'd be coming."

"I'm the only one who knew that," Eric said. "And they weren't my welcoming party."

"We'd expect a better party from you," Joe quipped.

"Did you log the information about our arrival in your computer files?" Frank asked, knowing the answer would be yes. Where else would a highly organized computer freak keep his calendar?

Eric hesitated a moment, then nodded.

"Did you talk to anyone about it?" Frank persisted.

"I cleared your visit with the project director," Eric replied, "but I didn't even tell her when I expected you. Security is pretty tight here. The guard had to contact me when you showed up, so I could vouch for you."

"What are you working on here?" Joe asked.

"Oh, the usual," Eric said. "Fish census and mapping, pollution checks, routine stuff. Why?"

"Our welcoming committee wanted some assurance that our dad wasn't involved in anything here," Frank replied.

Eric looked puzzled. "What would he be involved in here?"

"To the best of our knowledge, nothing," Joe answered. "But those guys thought differently."

The headset frequency they were using suddenly beeped. "Frank," Lowell said, cutting into their conversation, "I've had a call from the state police. They've come up empty-handed. I say it's time to take this bird home, too."

Frank spoke quickly to stop Joe from protesting. "We'll get back out here tomorrow and take a look at things ourselves."

"This is so cool!" Bess Marvin exclaimed for the hundredth time since getting off the train in Chicago's Union Station.

Nancy reminded her best friend, for the hundredth time, "Going on this cruise could also be dangerous, Bess. You do understand that, don't you?"

"Yes, Mother," Bess teased. "But that's not stopping either of us, is it?"

As soon as Nancy had returned to her hotel room early that morning, she called Bess, asking her to come along on the *Titanic* cruise. She had known that Bess wouldn't turn down her invitation. Their friendship meant a lot, but Bess probably would have said yes to her worst enemy for the chance at such a hot cruise, not to mention getting to meet Walter Welsch.

"Do you know how many people would kill to go where we're going to be?" Bess asked, lifting down her fourth bag from the train steps.

Nancy's shock must have showed on her face. That was what had happened the night before.

"Oops," Bess said. "That was a figure of speech. I wasn't thinking."

Nancy forced a smile. "It's okay." She put her arm around her friend's shoulder. "Am I ever glad you said yes. I can't think of anyone I'd rather be on a cruise with."

"Let's do it, girl!" Bess fluffed her straw blond hair with a hand and it obediently fell back into place, appearing freshly styled. Looking pretty was one of Bess's talents, given her full figure, sparkling eyes, and taste for anything new and different. She had turned more than a few heads getting off the train in her fitted yellow and white mini sundress.

"I can't believe the thought to turn down a free cruise from *the* Walter Welsch even entered your mind."

"It did, though," Nancy assured her. She glanced meaningfully at the four bags at their feet. "Is this all of it?"

"Yes." Bess hefted two of the bags. "I hardly had time to throw a wardrobe together and figured we'd go shopping for the rest here in Chicago. Are you parked nearby?"

Nancy nodded. Both girls knew their way around Chicago.

"Did you get hold of George to let her know about the cruise?" Nancy asked, falling into step beside Bess, after grabbing the other two pieces of luggage.

George Fayne was Bess's cousin. Nancy, Bess, and George had been inseparable growing up. Now they still spent a great deal of time with one another, though their different interests took them separate ways at times.

"I called her," Bess said. "I even talked to her briefly before the cell phone dead zone overtook her. What with her being far off the beaten path in the Grand Canyon, it's a surprise I got through to her at all." She dropped her bags and ran for a luggage trolley. "Let's travel in style," she said, pushing the cart back to Nancy.

"What is George doing in the Grand Canyon?" Nancy asked as they zipped through the crowds. She felt as if she'd been away for a year rather than a week.

"Remember when she applied to be a camp counselor for Teens in Jeopardy?" Bess asked.

Nancy remembered. She had written a letter of recommendation for George. They were at the exit across from where Nancy had parked her rental car. "The program was designed to help teenagers who had already had a number of brushes with the law. Kids could sign up for the white water rafting camp instead of weekly counseling sessions in the summer."

"That's the one," Bess said as she tossed her bags in the trunk of the car.

"But she didn't get the job," Nancy said. She'd been the one George had called in tears about it.

"Well, two days ago, a position opened up. They called George to see if she could fill it, and she flew out there yesterday," Bess explained.

Nancy slid behind the steering wheel and started the car. She left the door open for a moment till the air conditioner had a chance to chase the summer heat out of the car. After the temporary cooling effects of last night's storm, the city was frying once again in temperatures near one hundred degrees.

Bess immediately flipped down the passenger visor to check her face in the mirror. "George was not a happy camper when I told her about the cruise. But she was gracious enough to wish us bon voyage."

Nancy put the car in gear and followed the ramps out to the highway toward the Loop, which was Chicago's downtown area. "She'll get over it," she assured Bess. "After a night sleeping in a below decks cabin and a day without being able to get off the ship, George would be climbing the walls. She'd be much happier in the water than on it."

Bess returned to a favored subject. "You did mention something about shopping," she prompted. "Can we stop at Water Tower Place before we go to the hotel?"

"I have to go to the hotel first," Nancy said. "I've got some files to organize."

"That sounds a lot like work," Bess said suspiciously.

"There is a certain resemblance," Nancy admitted.

"What are these files?" Bess asked.

"A number of documents I downloaded from the Internet last night," Nancy answered. "They're all articles about Walter Welsch."

"Why do you want to read those?" Bess frowned as she pursued the subject.

"Because we're going on the cruise he offered us for free," Nancy replied, "and because I think there's more to Walter Welsch than I've had a chance to see."

"Whatever else there can be, it can't be anything but good," Bess declared. "Have you ever noticed that smile of his when he's interviewed on television? A guy with a smile that great can't be bad."

"I just don't think I'm getting the whole story from him," Nancy said.

"What's bothering you about him?" Bess asked, her interest finally piqued.

"Primarily," Nancy admitted, "the fact that he showed up at the police station so quickly after everything happened last night."

"I thought he explained that. He was watching television when the news broke."

"New York is his usual base of operations. What was he doing in Chicago?"

"He was probably on hand for the radio ticket giveaway." Bess raised an arched eyebrow. "You could always ask him."

Nancy pulled into the underground parking garage at the hotel. Everything Bess was saying made sense. She'd already had the same arguments with herself. But she also had a healthy respect for her intuition. And her intuition had questions. Why was Walter Welsch keeping secrets?

"And why should he personally come to the police station?" Nancy countered as she pulled into an open spot. "He has a lawyer and a public relations staff the size of a small army. It would seem more likely that one of them would show up for him."

Bess shrugged. "I don't have any answers."

"Neither do I, and that's what really bothers me." Nancy looked hard at her friend. "I would really appreciate some help getting those articles organized."

"And I just wanted to go shopping for a measly few hours." Bess sighed for sympathy.

"Okay," Nancy said, "I've got a deal. Let's go up to the room and work for a couple of hours. Let's say until one-thirty—then we'll go to lunch—my treat. After that we'll go shopping."

Reluctantly, Bess agreed.

After Bess had a chance to clean up, they

started on the stacks of paper Nancy had left all over the room.

They broke for lunch at one-thirty and walked to a nearby Greek restaurant that was a local favorite. From the cucumbers and yogurt on good Greek bread to the honey-drenched baklava for dessert, every mouthful revived Bess's flagging spirits. She was in a great shopping mood again by the time they reached the hotel to freshen up.

"We really don't have much in the way of cruise wear," Bess said, brushing her hair. "I watched some news footage on CNN this morning after your call. It was all about cruises. They ran footage aboard Welsch's ocean liner, which reminded me of all the opportunities we don't want to miss there."

"Oh, really," Nancy said, smiling in spite of her fatigue. "And just what opportunities could you be talking about?" As if she didn't know.

"Those white uniforms the cruise staff wear made me think how great a shipboard romance would be. I admit I get goose bumps just thinking about it." She put her brush down, grabbed her purse, and led the way to the door.

"Oh, *those* opportunities," Nancy said.

"Shipboard romance. It's music to my ears." Bess put her hand on the doorknob. "I, personally, can do without all the mystery you're looking for. That band of thieves you're hoping to find is probably long gone by now." She opened the door but stopped dead.

A hard-faced man filled the doorway. He wore a brown bomber jacket, charcoal pants, weathered riding boots, and a caramel-colored beret.

He held a small black pistol in a gloved hand pointed straight at Bess's heart.

Chapter

Eight

FINISHING UP a chess game with someone in Rangoon?" came a voice from the doorway.

Frank didn't have to look to know it was Joe. "Just some E-mail. I won that chess game before we left Bayport."

"Yeah, right." Joe sat on the edge of the bed, his hair still wet from a shower. He stifled a yawn and then stretched his arms above his head, separating each and every vertebra along his spine. "I'm still sore from last night."

"You're lucky you're feeling anything at all," Frank replied. "When that guy had you in his sights, I thought it was all over."

Joe gave a cocky grin. "I was too quick for him."

"It must be your mutant abilities." Frank closed the computer down. He gave a deep sigh.

"I'd love to know what all that was about last night."

"No kidding," Joe agreed. "Oh, I talked to Eric this morning. He's going to requisition a Jeep from the institute for us to use. Cool, huh?"

"When do we get it?"

Joe grinned at his brother. "First thing after breakfast."

"Meet you in the kitchen after I shower," Frank said. He stepped into the bathroom.

"You showered last night," Joe reminded him.

"If you'd gone for a swim in that pond, you'd be showering every chance you got, too," came Frank's reply as he turned on the hot water.

"Good morning, sleepyhead," Eric Cox greeted Joe in his booming voice from the kitchen.

"Sleepyhead?" Joe argued. "I'll have you know I was up before Frank this morning."

"Call the newspapers," Eric teased. He stood in front of an institutional-size range.

The kitchen took up one end of the large dining room. All the institute staff pitched in to prepare meals, and Eric had volunteered to make one of his famous breakfasts.

Joe didn't notice much of the decor or the windows that looked out over the docks. The thing he noticed first, as always, was the slim brunette seated at one end of the table. All the rest of the people at the table were men.

Joe steered himself to a chair directly across

from her. She wore a loose denim shirt over a midnight blue bikini. Her dark hair curled in just a little at her well tanned jawline. Joe estimated her age as twenty-something.

"Hi," he said, "shouldn't we meet?"

The girl arched her left eyebrow as she gazed at him over her coffee cup. "I believe we already have," she said coolly.

"It must have been in a past life," Joe suggested.

"Well, then," the girl said, getting up from the table, "it hasn't been long enough." She put her coffee cup in the sink on her way out.

"Wow," Eric said as soon as she was gone. "That was Mandy's quickest brush-off yet."

The men at the table behind them laughed in agreement.

Joe got up and helped himself to coffee. "You think that was a brush-off? No way. She was just letting me know she was interested."

"Using that kind of energy right before breakfast has to have made you hungry," Eric said, waving a spatula. "I've got sausage-and-egg burritos, and there's a melon salad in the fridge."

"Sounds good." Joe spied the stack of tortillas on a plate next to the range. "How many do you have?"

"I'll keep them coming," Eric promised.

"You always struck me as a smart man," Joe said by way of thanks.

Joe glanced at the four men at the table as he sat down. One of them was Norman Lowell, the institute's security chief, whom he'd met the night before.

"Eric," a heavy-set bald man said in a German accent, "you should introduce us to this young man."

Eric did the honors with his back to the table, busily assembling breakfast burritos. "Dietrich, Coker, Ventura, this is Joe Hardy. Joe, meet Dietrich—assistant director here—Coker—a diver extraordinaire—and Ventura—who is curious about last night. He's a diver, too."

Ventura held his forefinger and thumb about an inch apart and grinned. "Well, maybe a little. Intrigue is such a nice addition to most lives, don't you think?"

"In measured doses," Joe agreed. "Last night was overkill."

"Fortunately," Dietrich said, "that is only an expression this morning."

Eric set a tray of sausage-and-egg burritos and melon salad on the table.

Joe helped himself to two burritos and a bowl of melon. He dug in with gusto.

"Who was that girl who was so obviously interested in me?" Joe asked. "She said I'd already met her."

"Mandy MacMahon," Coker said.

"The girl on the phone last night?" Joe called out to the chef.

"That's right," Eric called back.

"A word of advice, young Joe," Dietrich said.

"My favorite thing for breakfast," Joe said.

"I shall give it anyway." Dietrich smiled. "I am sure Miss MacMahon would rather be thought of as a young woman, not a girl. She spent a tour in the United States Air Force before the institute was fortunate enough to acquire her services."

"She is a genius with a Klein side-scan sonar," Ventura added.

"And she can handle nearly any vessel above or below the water," Coker said.

"She also," Dietrich said, cleaning his glasses, "gives one the impression that she is quite content to pursue her own course—alone."

Joe smiled broadly at this barrage of "advice."

"Ooooh," a new voice said. "Is sis about to break the heart of a young new target?"

Turning around, Joe saw a giant of a young man stride through the doorway. He looked like an Olympic athlete in running shorts, an expensive pair of track shoes, and a purple muscle shirt with an American flag patch on the front.

He stood at least six feet eight inches tall and had sun-streaked sandy blond hair. He was fair complected in spite of his burnished gold tan.

"Meet Oliver MacMahon," Eric said. "Mandy's brother. Oliver, this is Joe."

"Pleased to meet you, Joe." The giant's hand engulfed Joe's.

"Finished with your run?" Eric asked.

"Yeah." Oliver patted the flat planes of his stomach. "Now that I've done my duty, I'm ready for a cholesterol intake."

"Never have I seen a young man so willing to work his body just so he can abuse it." Dietrich shook his head. "If you're going to exercise so, you should watch your diet. If your diet is going to be such a horror, then you should give up running and exercising."

"I'm stubborn." Oliver grinned. "So far, I can't give up either."

Eric gave him a plate overflowing with food. He looked at Joe. "He's the only guy I know that can eat more than you."

"I'm still growing," Oliver protested.

"You're not that much older than I am, are you?" Joe asked.

"Depends on how old you are," Oliver replied with a big grin. "Twenty-four. The same as Mandy."

"You're really her brother?" Joe asked, making sure that this Hercules wasn't competition.

"More than that. I'm her twin."

"No way," Joe responded with a modicum of surprise but more relief.

"Way," Oliver said. "Fraternal twins, of course. It's really crazy what genetics can do. Mandy takes after my dad. I'm more like my mom."

Joe took another cup of coffee. "So what do you do here?"

"I'm one of the divers. I work with Coker."

Coker nodded. "He's not telling all of it. Oliver is an accomplished marine biologist, and one of our most gifted sailors."

Oliver blushed and concentrated on his food.

Coker got up from the table with his coffee and walked to the windows overlooking the coast.

Dietrich sat placidly watching the young men and sipping coffee.

Joe pushed his plate away in surrender. His thoughts were already out the door, running to the site of their attack and then returning to Mandy MacMahon.

"Hey," Coker said. "Somebody has a problem out there in a boat. There's smoke."

Joe joined everyone else at the window.

Out on the rolling curve of the ocean, a motorboat with sails struggled to get out of the harbor. The sails blossomed, full of wind, while smoke poured out of the engine area.

From the black color of the smoke rising into the sky, Joe knew that it was an oil-based fire.

In the next instant, the boat blew up in an orange ball of flame and debris.

Chapter

Nine

THE SONIC BOOM of the explosion rattled the window against Joe Hardy's palms. He watched in horror as a mushroom of black smoke and orange flames billowed up from the stricken motor sailer toward the cerulean blue sky.

"Mandy!" Oliver MacMahon screamed, and bolted from the room.

Joe took off in pursuit, figuring Oliver knew the quickest way to the coastline. They twisted through the corridors of the dorm, meeting Frank along the way.

"I thought I heard an explosion," Frank said.

"You did," Joe replied. His brother fell in beside him. Both of them found themselves hard pressed to keep up with Oliver.

Oliver slammed through the front doors, letting in the morning sunshine and opening a view

to the coastline. Frank grabbed a fire extinguish-
er from the wall, and Joe picked up a braided rug
in front of the door that was a yard wide and two
yards long.

Out in the water, the motor sailer foundered
quickly.

"She's taking on water too fast!" Frank yelled.
"Whatever blew must have gone off near the
waterline."

Oliver ran out onto one of the docks and cast
off the line of one of the powerboats. He had the
engines started by the time Joe joined him.

"Take the next one!" Oliver yelled to Frank.
"The keys are in it. We'll need the space."

Joe checked the storage area under the seats
and came up with six neon orange life jackets.
He tossed them into a loose pile in the center of
the boat. Salty spray sluiced up over the prow of
the powerboat and stung his eyes.

In less than a minute, they had arrived at the
damaged boat. Joe tossed three of the life jackets
out to the survivors he spotted in the water.

"How many aboard the motor sailer?" he
asked Oliver.

"Should be eleven." Oliver cut the powerboat's throttle. It responded at once, losing
speed. "They were supposed to check some sonar
sites. Man, whoever did this is going to pay."

Joe stared at the burning wreckage. Two more
survivors swam nearby. One of them moved
weakly, blood glistening on her head before the

next wave washed it away. Joe threw them life jackets, too.

"Mandy would have been below," Oliver yelled over the grim crackle of the flames. "That's where all the research instruments are."

Surveying the burning husk of the boat, Joe didn't see how anyone could have survived the explosion. A huge hole gaped on the starboard side. Curiously, flames twisted inside the hole despite the water that rushed in to fill the below-decks area.

Joe dipped the rug he'd picked up into the roiling sea. It came up feeling leaden in his hands.

The powerboat bumped up against the much bigger motor sailer, jerking randomly. Joe grabbed the hull of the bigger boat to steady himself. He slung the last life preserver over one arm, then grabbed the wet carpet.

"This isn't going to buy us much time," Joe said.

Oliver nodded, stretching up to lash a line to the motor sailer. "I've got to find Mandy."

"Tying us to the motor sailer might not be a good idea," Joe announced. "When it goes down, it could take us with it."

"Then we're going to have to be back—with Mandy—before that happens, aren't we?"

Joe grabbed the side of the motor sailer and hoisted himself up. The metal of the bigger boat held almost enough heat to sear his palms. He clambered aboard, then slapped the wet carpet down across the deck in front of him.

Water from the carpet sprayed across the deck, extinguishing flames and leaving a path. Joe slapped the carpet down again, soaking another section of the deck. In this way, it took him three more wet slaps to reach the hatch where a companionway led down.

From above, Joe could see a man hunkered down in the walkway. His face held a grimace of pain. "Help," he called out. "I'm down here. I think my leg's broken."

The man reached up. Joe scrambled down below and took the man's arm before hefting him into a fireman's carry across his shoulders. "This is going to hurt some," he apologized.

"A little hurt I can take," the man said. "It's better than burning to death."

"If I put you down in the water with the life jacket," Joe asked, "do you think you can make it away from here?"

"Watch me," the man said.

Joe helped the man pull the life jacket into place and fasten the straps. Balancing the man's weight, Joe leaned over the side of the motor sailer and controlled the man's fall into the sea. He held on to the man's arm as long as he could, then released him.

The man gave Joe a painful thumbs-up and started swimming slowly away under his own power.

Joe started back downstairs. Gritting his teeth against the pain in his hands from the heated rug, Joe seized it and began slapping it against the door at the end of the passageway.

The door held.

He stepped back and drove his foot against the door jamb. The lock shattered, falling from its housing in a handful of pieces.

Fortunately, no backdraft came rushing out at him. He went inside, barely able to see through the dense, dark smoke. His eyes burned as he scanned the workroom.

Computers and other electronic gear occupied workstations on built-in desks. High-pierced keening echoed within the room. Small red lights flashed in warning.

Joe pressed forward, staring into the smoke. He found a window by touch, then confirmed it by pressing his face against the glass. Inset high on the wall, the window normally afforded a view over the motorsailer's bow.

Fumbling for the lock, Joe shoved the window open. Some of the smoke immediately trailed out. At the same time, small waves of water splashed in through the window.

Joe turned away and a feeling of vertigo suddenly assailed him. At first he thought it was because of a lack of oxygen, then he realized what it was. The boat was listing dramatically.

Before Joe recovered, a deluge of water roared in through the open window. He slipped and fell, instantly drenched. In seconds, inches of water eddied and swirled around his ankles, already climbing to his calves.

The boat was sinking faster and faster.

Frank worked with the other powerboat's lines. Two of them secured the craft to the dock, and he couldn't get them loose. He no longer heard the rattle of the powerboat Oliver MacMahon piloted.

All around him, chaos spun out. The roar of a Jeep pulling onto the dock drowned out the sound of the voices screaming to one another.

The dock vibrated as footsteps raced along it. Frank stared hard at the shiny veneer covering the mooring lines. He realized that a quick-set glue coated the lines, bonding them to the dock rings.

"What's the problem?" a harsh voice demanded.

Frank saw institute security chief, Norman Lowell, standing above him, glaring down. "Someone's glued the dock lines."

Lowell pulled a lock-back knife from his belt. "Start the engines. I'll get the ropes."

Frank switched the ignition key on. The engines rumbled to life, sending vibrations through the powerboat.

Lowell raked his knife across the mooring lines. The ropes parted easily as the knife's keen edge flashed in the morning sun. The security chief dropped into the powerboat. "Go!"

Frank threw the engines into reverse and

backed the powerboat out. Then he shoved the throttles forward. The powerboat surged ahead, the force of its takeoff shoving them back in their seats.

Lowell held on to the short windscreen in front of them. His chiseled features reflected calm, but Frank read the man's body language and knew the security chief was anything but relaxed.

Frank felt the same way. Despite the clouds of smoke surrounding the doomed motor sailer, he spotted eight survivors, all treading water easily. They'd have to wait to be picked up on the return trip. The powerboat Joe and Oliver had taken, he could make out, was tied up to the motor sailer.

Fewer than sixty yards away, Frank was closing on the motor sailer when another explosion suddenly rocked the boat, ripping it in two. A huge gust of flames shot skyward.

Before Frank had time to react to the debris falling through the sky, the motor sailer disappeared under the cool jade water.

In seconds only white foam and charred debris remained to mark the spot where the boat had gone down. A few of the floating pieces were still aflame.

Frank felt himself go numb, but he didn't pause. He and Joe led lives filled with uncertainty and danger; they made their own luck in the face of adversity. He scanned the water. The debris on the surface and the smoke in the air made it hard to see clearly.

"Over there," Lowell shouted, pointing.

Frank followed the line of the security chief's finger. A dark-haired young woman surfaced in a semicircle of burning planks. Her face was covered with soot.

Frank quickly but carefully steered toward her. Lowell leaned down over the side and helped her aboard.

"Are you okay?" the security chief asked.

"Yes." The woman came forward to the cockpit and stared out into the water with wide eyes. She wrapped her arms around herself, visibly shaken. Stains covered her torn, drenched clothing. "Have you found all of the others?" Her voice cracked as she spoke.

"You're the ninth we've spotted," Frank answered.

"Two are still missing," she stated.

"More than that," Frank replied grimly. "My brother and someone else from the institute had reached the motor sailer and tried to rescue the people aboard it."

The young woman turned to Lowell, a worried expression on her smudged face. "Who?"

Lowell hesitated for a moment. "Oliver."

"Oh no!" The woman turned back to the water, glancing at Frank. "Get moving. We can't just sit here. We have to find my brother!"

"Mandy," Lowell said, sitting by her, "I'm sorry."

"Oliver wasn't supposed to be on that boat," Mandy stated.

"I know." Lowell squeezed her shoulder reassuringly. "I tried to stop him, but Oliver had a big lead. He was gone before I could get to him."

Frank knew how the woman felt as he stared into the smoke-shrouded water. Even though the boat had disappeared, the smoke remained, obscuring their view. He turned to look at Lowell and spotted the institute helicopter in the sky over the security chief's shoulder.

"Get the helicopter over here," Frank suggested. "The backdraft from the rotors might blow the smoke off."

"It's worth a try." Lowell contacted the helicopter team on a walkie-talkie and ordered the aircraft in.

Frank waited impatiently, wondering how long Joe had been under or if he was under. The seconds stretched into the next minute.

Joe floated in stillness under the ocean's surface. His senses swam, turning on a kaleidoscopic light show around him. He wasn't sure how far down he was, but he knew from the pressure in his ears that he had reached an uncomfortable depth.

The motor sailer had broken into pieces, and he was now being pulled upward in the wake of one of them. He knew somehow that he'd break the surface unharmed.

All at once he spotted Oliver MacMahon below him. The man appeared to be unconscious, caught in a tangle of sailcloth and mast lines.

Joe struck out at once, diving after Oliver. His

lungs began to burn from lack of oxygen by the time he reached him. He fished a pocketknife out of his shorts and sawed at the lines now dragging both of them down.

When the last strand of rope parted, Joe grabbed Oliver under the chin and swam up with him. He watched the last pieces of the motor sailer disappear into the darkness of the depths below.

Joe glanced up at the surface, which seemed very far away. His lungs felt as if they were about to collapse. It took every bit of his concentration and will power not to open his mouth to breathe.

Chapter

Ten

WOULD YOU MIND stepping back, love? Just a wee bit, if you please. Don't go thinking about bolting and running. This doesn't have to be unpleasant for any of us."

A wicked silencer stuck out from the muzzle of the small pistol pointed at Bess.

Fear exploded through Nancy as she recognized the man from the data she'd seen at the police department. He was Chauncey Forsythe, one of the ex–intelligence agents working with Amos Jericho, the rogue CIA agent. According to the little she remembered from Detective Reynolds's file, Forsythe had been with Britain's MI-6 agency before throwing in with Jericho.

"Do as he says," Nancy told Bess quietly. She reached out for her friend's arm and gently guided her back into the hotel room. She was well aware that there was no means of escape from the room. She'd have to use her wits to get out of this.

Bess backed up. Still, she wasn't about to give up without a fight. "This is a very busy hotel," she said. "If I screamed right now, do you think you'd get away before security caught you?"

The man flashed her an amused but cold grin. His light gray eyes resembled glacial ice. "I guess the question you need to ask yourself, love, is whether you and your friend would be around to find out."

Angry sparks jumped in Bess's blue eyes.

"If I wished you any ill will, it would have already happened," Forsythe said.

"Bess," Nancy coaxed gently. She kept pulling her friend back into the room.

"There's a smart lass. Now, common sense is something we can all appreciate." Forsythe waved the pistol. "Please have a seat on that bed."

Nancy and Bess sat down on the edge of Nancy's bed. "What do you want?" Nancy demanded.

"Just to have a few questions answered, love. That's all."

Despite his calm demeanor, Nancy sensed uncertainty in the man. Who comes asking questions with a pistol?

Forsythe had a narrow face framed by small muttonchop whiskers that had not been in his British intelligence photographs. Curly brown hair streaked with gray poked out from under his beret.

"What questions?" Nancy asked.

Removing his beret, Forsythe kept it clutched in one hand. "I want to talk about your night last night."

Nancy didn't see that she had any choice. He didn't seem interested in Trey Carter, but he wanted to know everything about Amos Jericho.

"So no one actually saw Jericho last night?" Chauncey Forsythe asked.

"No," Nancy answered. "But the FBI identified him immediately from the video. After all, they were already looking for him."

Forsythe looked up in surprise. "Why?"

Nancy felt stupid. Why did I say that? I may have to answer his questions, but I don't have to volunteer information. She explained about the robbery in California.

The news made the man nervous. He ran a forefinger across his lips. "Very interesting, love," he growled, preoccupied. "It's not like old Amos to run with a new crowd. Always a cautious one, he was. Never met a man more likely to have grown eyes in the back of his skull."

"So you haven't seen Amos Jericho for a while?" Nancy asked.

Forsythe fixed her with his chilly gaze. "You're a sharp one, lass, aren't you."

"But you've been in contact with Jericho, haven't you?" Nancy pressed, pleased that her own blunder had been rewarded in kind. "Otherwise you wouldn't be here now, and you wouldn't be asking these questions."

"Why I'm asking these questions is nobody's business but my own, and you'd do well to remember that. If I were you, m'girl, I'd forget we ever had this little conversation." Forsythe started for the door, keeping Bess and Nancy covered with his pistol. "I'll see myself out. Don't bother getting up. And I mean don't bother for, say, the next ten minutes."

He received no answer.

"There's a love. Ta." Forsythe exited.

"That creep!" Bess exploded as the door closed. She bolted from the bed toward the door.

"Wait, Bess!" Nancy cried. She caught Bess's arm. "Wait."

"He'll get away," Bess argued.

"And if we catch him?" Nancy asked.

Bess didn't answer.

"If we catch him, Bess, he'll kill us."

"That's eleven," Norman Lowell announced as the final member of the crew was hauled out of the water. The only people left unaccounted for were Joe and Oliver.

The institute's helicopter flew into position overhead. As Frank had thought, the draft from the aircraft's whirling rotor blades thinned the smoke hovering over the water. He gazed up into the helicopter's cargo area, surprised to see Eric Cox step into the doorway wearing a scuba tank.

Eric grabbed the mouthpiece and fitted it into

place as the helicopter dropped to within a few feet of the ocean surface. A moment later he flipped gracefully into the water and disappeared. Two other divers followed.

When the water above him suddenly roiled and bubbled in such straight lines, Joe had a brief hallucinatory impression that he'd been depth charged. Then he realized that the projectiles blasting through the ocean above him weren't depth charges at all. He recognized Eric Cox in the forefront of the divers.

In seconds the three divers surrounded Oliver and Joe. Two of them took Oliver, who was starting to wake up. Eric took Joe's arm and held his scuba mouthpiece out to him. Joe breathed deeply into the mouthpiece, never so grateful for plain old oxygen. Using the buddy system, he and Eric swam for the surface.

"Finding you two turned out to be pretty easy," Eric announced.

"I'm glad you think so," Frank responded, "because I couldn't see anything." He piloted the powerboat back toward the institute. Every seat was taken. Joe, Oliver, and Eric sat on the floor while other survivors took up the seats.

"It wasn't about seeing anything," Eric said. "It was about hearing."

Mandy MacMahon stood behind Oliver, a towel draped over her head and shoulders. "The coastline here is dotted with sonar beacons. All Eric had to do was tap into the regular feeds, get a fix on this location, and do a quick search."

Frank felt certain it was harder than Mandy had described. It had also taken a lot of quick thinking on their friend's behalf. Frank mentally kicked himself. Sonar was part of the environment he and Joe were in now. He felt he should have thought of it as well.

"Right," Eric said in a voice that betrayed his irritation. Frank could think of no other reason for his friend's reaction than that he'd lost the opportunity to tell his own rescue story. "We've even got a fix on the motor sailer's wreckage," he continued. "We may be able to hoist it up and look for clues to what happened."

Frank glanced at Mandy. "Do you have any idea what happened?"

"No. I was below working on the sonar array system that I wanted to set up for the pictures we were going to take. All at once I felt a vibration. Really nothing, I thought."

"It felt as if the bottom of the motor sailer scraped across a submerged log," Hans Johanson, the man who had broken his leg, stated. He had his leg propped up on a metal specimen case from the storage area. "That happens in these waters every so often. Harbor patrols usually haul the logs out, but they don't get them all."

Other crew members agreed.

"Then the explosion ripped the middle of the

boat out," Mandy said. "I was below when it happened. I managed to swim through the cargo hold and get out."

"The final explosion blew the motor sailer away," Joe finished.

"It must have been the engines," Hans stated. "Something must have caused them to blow."

"Those engines were in good shape," Oliver said defensively. "I checked them."

"No one said you didn't." Mandy soothed her brother by putting her hand on his shoulder "Mistakes happen."

Oliver nodded morosely.

Frank caught Joe's eye, telegraphing his thinking. Joe nodded almost imperceptibly. Neither one of them believed that the explosions had come from the engines. The first bump that had been felt was probably the initial explosion that disabled the steering section and opened the underside of the boat. With no steering, the motor sailer had settled into the water and was set up for the final kill.

A group of institute personnel rushed forward to meet them as they reached the docks. The wounded were strapped onto stretchers, hauled out of the boat, and rushed to the institute's clinic. From there, a few—including Hans Johanson—would be flown by helicopter to the local hospital.

As Frank and Joe helped crew members out of the boat, a blue institute Jeep roared up to a stop.

The tires spat out small rocks as the brakes grabbed.

A tall woman unfolded herself from behind the steering wheel and stepped onto the running board. She wore khaki pants and a blue denim workshirt with the sleeves rolled up to mid-forearm. Her thick salt-and-pepper hair hung to her shoulders. Oval-shaped glasses accentuated her green eyes, which were narrowed in anger or maybe indignation.

Frank thought it might be both.

"Mandy," the woman said, striding up to within inches of the MacMahon twins, "what happened to that boat?"

Mandy gently put her hand on the woman's arm. "I can't honestly say, Libby, but I believe something in the engine room exploded."

"It was sabotage," Lowell announced. "I heard at least one explosion myself."

The woman's face became even more set. She turned away and looked out into the harbor. "Walter Welsch isn't going to get away with this!"

Chapter

Eleven

JOE RECOGNIZED the billionaire's name at once and caught Frank's eye.

"Libby," Mandy said calmly, "you don't know that Welsch had anything to do with this."

Anger tightened the woman's jawline. "Yes, I do."

Eric drew close to Frank and Joe. "Libby McCarthy," he said in a hushed voice. "She's the project director."

Libby waded into the ocean, her fists shoved deep in her pants pockets. Gentle waves rolled in over her sandaled feet. "Norman?" she called out without turning around. "Did you shoot any film of the accident?"

"No, Libby." Lowell shook his head. Mirror sunglasses covered his eyes, shooting off sparks from the morning sun. "It was a rescue mission."

"Well, get some now."

Lowell nodded and lifted his walkie-talkie. "They've got cameras aboard the helicopters," he said to no one in particular. He issued swift commands over the handset.

"Burke," Libby said.

"Yes, ma'am." A grizzled, pot-bellied man stepped out of the crowd. His skin shone dark bronze from a lifetime of working on the water.

"I want a boat out there with a dredge as soon as possible, and I want a salvage crew working that site until we get some answers."

"Yes, ma'am."

Libby shook her head at the ocean and finally turned around, noticing Frank and Joe for the first time.

"Eric," she said, "introduce me to your friends."

Eric did as he was told.

"Rather more of an exciting introduction to the institute than we'd anticipated," Libby said. "I'm glad neither of you was injured."

Joe nodded, wondering how best to frame his question. He had to accept the fact that no matter how he put it, he was going to sound pushy. "What makes you think Walter Welsch had anything to do with what happened to that boat?"

"Because Walter Welsch knows how I feel about his raising the *Titanic,*" the woman responded. "Fifteen hundred people died in that tragedy, and they've been resting there for almost ninety years. They should be left in peace."

Joe listened to the conviction in her voice, but it still didn't explain her thinking.

"Libby's planning a demonstration," Eric said, filling them in. "She and Walter used to be"—he fumbled for the correct term—"friends."

"Yes, we were," Libby stated. "Good friends. I'd always thought he was a compassionate man until he set out to do this thing. In the last few months, I've discovered to what lengths Walter will go to achieve his ends."

Joe felt immediate sympathy for Libby. The hurt in her voice, though masked, sounded raw and recent.

"What kind of demonstration?" Frank asked.

"You know about the cruise up to the *Titanic* on Welsch's ocean liner, the *Hampton?*" Eric asked.

"Yes," Frank replied. Who in the country hadn't heard about it?

"Walter auctioned off the rights to televise his footage of raising the *Titanic* to one of the networks. Not only is he getting paid quite handsomely for his grave robbing, but the whole world will get to be titillated by the event."

"But anyone can film it from satellites and other ships," Joe pointed out.

"But what will they get?" Libby asked. "Unless they have access to a submersible, such as we have here, they'll only get shots near the surface and above." Then, as if talking to herself, she added, "The only plan I could come up with was to offer our film to public TV for nothing."

"Libby's talking about our submersible, the *Manta,*" Eric interjected.

Joe remembered Eric had mentioned that they'd be able to get a close look at the three-person deep-diving pod.

"The *Manta,*" Libby announced, "was the first thing Walter tried to sabotage."

Standing in the large warehouse, Frank Hardy stared at the submersible in front of him.

The *Manta* was about the size of a college dorm room, some twenty feet long and ten feet high. The prow blossomed out like an opaque bubble. Robot arms with huge claws stuck out from beneath the prow along with some very specialized camera equipment.

"It looks like a giant lobster," Joe cracked.

Libby McCarthy smiled, which erased a few of the worry lines on her face. "But this is one sturdy crustacean." She pointed at the prow. "That bubble is made of four-inch titanium and can carry a two-person crew with a passenger. She's cleared to dive to nearly twenty thousand feet. There are only a handful of submersibles in the world that can do that."

"And each foot of diving capability," Eric put in, "costs about a thousand dollars."

"That's twenty million dollars!" Frank exclaimed.

Eric nodded. "Even if you had the money to replace the *Manta,* you couldn't find one."

"I guess there isn't a used sub dealership on every corner," Joe said.

"Exactly," Libby replied emphatically. "And not many countries have the technology or economic resources to build a submersible like this. That's why Walter tried to sabotage it." Her cellular phone rang, taking her attention. She spoke rapidly, giving orders for the institute's search party.

Frank followed Joe and Eric as they walked under the submersible, but only after hearing Libby say that the state police would be there soon.

"The *Manta*'s not going to set any speed records," Eric stated, "but she gets around okay on the ocean floor. Once you get used to the controls, you'd be surprised how nimble those robot arms are."

"You've been down there?" Joe asked. He ran his hands along the sub's outer skin and peered in through a thick porthole.

"I've crewed aboard her three times," Eric answered. "If we get permission would you like to go down in her?"

"In a New York minute." Joe grinned in anticipation.

The prospect excited Frank as well, but he was keeping an ear on Libby's phone conversation.

"Man," Eric said, his eyes gleaming as he

patted the side of the submersible, "you only think you've been under the water until you get there in this baby. It's so dark down there that if you turned off the cabin lights, you couldn't see a hand in front of your face. We're talking about a real frontier experience."

Libby punched the cellular phone off and folded it up.

"You said Walter Welsch made an attempt to sabotage the *Manta,*" Frank said to her. "When was this?" The accusation against Welsch sounded farfetched.

"A month and four days ago," Libby answered.

"What happened?" Frank asked.

"A break-in, physical damage," Libby said. "Nothing sophisticated. Norman's staff tracked the saboteurs from the outer gates to this warehouse. His team stopped them from doing a thorough job."

"Was anyone caught?" Joe asked.

Libby shook her head. "Unfortunately, no. But one of our guards was shot and wounded."

Frank looked at Joe and Eric. "That doesn't sound like Walter Welsch's style," he said to the project director.

Libby's words dripped acid. "Walter has proven surprising in a number of ways." Then she added with less venom, "There are a number of people who would like to see him get a black eye over this."

Frank had read about the controversies—personal and professional—that Welsch's scheme had created. A man didn't reach Walter Welsch's stature without making enemies. As Frank studied the woman in front of him, he wondered which had come first—Libby McCarthy's decision to protest the raising of the *Titanic* or the break-up of her romance with the billionaire.

He passed on asking that particular question. "How do you know Welsch was behind the attempt on the *Manta?*"

"During the confusion," Libby answered, "a security camera in the hangar got a picture of one of the men. All of them were masked, but Lowell got his hands on one of them and succeeded in unmasking him."

"You identified the man?" Joe asked.

"Not really. Norman didn't actually see the man. All he knows is he came away with a mask and very nearly got shot."

"Well, what about the tape?" Frank wanted to know.

Libby scowled. "I had the security tape in the safe in my office. When I turned it over to the police, we found it had been degaussed. Without the tape, we didn't have anything."

Degaussing with a powerful magnet, Frank knew, would totally eradicate anything captured on the tape.

"Why didn't someone just steal the tape if he got close enough to degauss it?" Joe asked.

"I think Walter wanted to remind me how powerless I was to stop him," Libby said.

"Did you talk to him?" Frank asked.

"It didn't do any good. He denied everything. I was surprised he even took my call."

"Could we take a look at the file?" Frank asked.

"Sure. I don't know that it would do any good." Libby fixed him with a hopeful stare. "I've heard that your father is a good detective. Do you think he would be interested in investigating this?"

"He's on assign—" Frank began, but Eric cut him off.

"What would you want with one Hardy when you could get two?" Eric said. "Second to their old man, they're the best there is."

Joe, Frank, and Eric left as soon as the police had taken their statements. They had another investigation to work on.

Joe was grateful that the breeze coming in from the coast was cool as he searched the area where he and Frank had been attacked. Even with the breeze, looking for any clue was hot and backbreaking work. He raked his gaze down the broken path their van had taken the night before.

Frank and Eric were working farther down the incline. Eric carried a metal detector, the long rod extending before him as he walked slowly through the marshy area. Frank moved along the shore of the pond, following the path he'd taken the night before. He could see the deep ruts where their van had been before being towed to the nearest garage that morning.

The only thing they'd found so far had been the collector's issue of the *X-Guardian* comic book they had brought for Eric. Amazingly, it had weathered the long night intact in its plastic sheath.

"You wouldn't expect any less from a super-hero with mutant abilities," Eric had cracked. They had all laughed, just what they needed after the morning's events.

Joe's mouth felt as if it had been annexed by a desert. He glanced halfway up the hill at the institute Jeep Eric had borrowed for their excursion. He lifted the walkie-talkie from its holster on his hip and pressed the talk button. "Hey, guys, I'm going to get something to drink. Do you want anything?"

"I'll be up in a minute," Eric replied.

"So will I," Frank said. "I've got something I want to show you."

"What is it?" Joe asked.

"I said I'd show you," Frank teased.

Joe took a pair of compact binoculars from his pocket and focused them on his brother. Frank had his back to him and was putting something in his pocket. Joe tried to focus on whatever it was but couldn't get the angle he needed.

He sighed and put the binoculars away. Only when his brother got ready to reveal whatever it was that he'd learned would Joe find out.

As Joe reached the Jeep and opened the cooler, he caught a flicker of movement along the edge of the trees to his right. He took out a bottle of water and had a long drink. The bottle would mask the shift of his gaze in case anyone was watching.

There was no further movement, but Joe did see a suspicious shadow. He opened up the frequency on his walkie-talkie again. "Hey, Frank, I'm beginning to think we're wasting our time out here." As he spoke, he lightly tapped a finger on the transmitter. Most anyone eavesdropping wouldn't have noticed that the seemingly distracted tapping was really Morse code for SOS.

Joe saw Frank turn and look up at him as he heard, "Well, don't give up."

"I'm not," Joe said. "I may try my luck farther up the hill, though." He began his upward climb, angling away from whoever was spying on them. "I'll let you know if I find anything."

"Do that."

Once he was sure he was out of sight of the spy, Joe broke into a run. He wove through the trees and brush almost silently. In seconds, he had doubled back down the hill and was coming up behind the shadow.

A man stood against a tree, his profile extended just beyond the bark. Taller than Joe, he appeared to be about as athletic. Unlike Joe, however, he had an automatic pistol in a shoulder holster.

Joe imagined he was one of the men who'd attacked them the night before. There was only one way to find out. He crept closer, getting almost within arm's reach.

Suddenly, in one smooth movement, the man turned, dropped into a crouch, and came up, aiming a roundhouse kick straight at Joe's face!

Chapter

Twelve

THE PAST THREE HOURS of shopping with Bess
had been strangely relaxing. Nancy had been
distracted from the unanswerable questions that
stuck in her mind. But now all of a sudden all the
clothes, the perfumes, and the constant chatter
of strangers threatened sensory overload.

Bess was in the fitting room and Nancy had
come out to find an evening wrap to go with the
dress she was thinking of buying. She stood
before a bank of mirrors wearing a short, deep
blue, strapless dress over which she had just
added a blue shawl with glittery gold threads
woven through it.

She gazed at the dress and shawl with a critical
eye. The dress was rather daring. Nancy shook
her head at her reflection.

"No, no, no," a masculine voice stated. "It

would be a crime to talk yourself out of that dress."

Startled, but not ready to embarrass herself by overreacting, Nancy looked coolly at the reflection in the mirror.

Over her shoulder, about ten feet behind her, stood Walter Welsch with his hands in his pockets. His smile was charming.

"Mr. Welsch," Nancy said, turning around. "Do you shop here often?"

The billionaire shook his head. "No."

"Then I take it our meeting here is not by chance," Nancy said.

Welsch didn't hesitate. "No, not by chance at all. I must confess that since our meeting last night, I've had a security team looking after you. We don't know what Jericho or one of his people might try to do, since he knows about your involvement in last night's incident." He smiled warmly.

Nancy was nonplussed. "That's an invasion of privacy."

"My apologies," Welsch responded. "I only had your best interests at heart."

Nancy dismissed his excuse, saying, "The words of any number of would-be dictators."

Welsch gave her a confused grin and pointed toward the entrance. "Maybe I should go out and try coming in again. I seem to have gotten off on the wrong foot."

Nancy sighed. "No, I should apologize. I've

been shopping too long. And this day hasn't gone exactly as planned."

"So I heard," Welsch replied.

Nancy gave him a surprised look.

"After seeing you safely to your hotel after lunch, my men waited for you in the lobby. I didn't want them going up with you and loitering in your hall, tipping you off. It was a mistake."

"Bess and I weren't hurt," Nancy said. Then she chuckled. "I haven't noticed your men all day. They must be very good."

"They are. I'm certain if they'd known of your situation, Mr. Forsythe wouldn't have gotten away."

Nancy nodded, ready to change the subject. "So what brings you here?"

Before Welsch could answer, Bess appeared at the far end of the aisle, strutting toward Nancy like a model on a runway.

Bess had almost reached Nancy when she recognized Welsch. She stopped in midslink and blushed fiercely.

Covering her own laughter at Bess's discomfort, Nancy quickly made the introductions.

"A lovely outfit, Ms. Marvin," Welsch complimented.

"Please, I'm too young to be Ms. Marvin." Bess shuddered. "Call me Bess."

"And I'm too young to be Mr. Welsch. Walter, please." He gazed at Nancy. "May I use your first name, Ms. Drew?"

"Of course," Nancy said. "But I'm not too young for anything!"

Their laughter broke the tension in the air.

"I was thinking of this for the cruise." Bess spun around.

"I'm enchanted that you're going to be joining us," Welsch said. "I've already reserved adjoining rooms for the two of you, and you'll have passes to any of the organized events you'd care to attend." He turned to face Nancy. "And that brings me to my reason for being here."

Bess looked from Welsch to Nancy and back. "Nothing's gone wrong with the cruise, has it?"

"Don't even think it," Welsch said emphatically. "After all this work, everything will go smoothly, I hope."

"So," Bess continued in her most disarming voice, "why are you here?"

"I would like the honor of taking you both to the Chicago launch of the *Hampton* tonight. It's a gala party at an art museum for all the backers, promoters, and passengers. Please say yes."

Bess shot an urgent yes glance at Nancy, and mouthed the words: "Society pages."

Nancy knew that Bess would wait for her to answer. She was of two minds about whether to accept. Of course, she'd love to go. What could be more fun than to be escorted by such a charming billionaire? Then again, this charming billionaire had put a tail on them. That not only made her mad, but it gave Welsch the edge while she was trying to investigate *him.*

"Why ask us?" Nancy inquired.

"Because you're my guests on the *Hampton,*" Welsch answered. "This will be only the first of many treats for you."

"Nancy, may I speak to you for a moment," Bess piped up. "Excuse us, Walter."

Nancy led Bess a few steps away for privacy, but Bess was too rattled to keep her voice down.

"Nancy," Bess whispered loudly enough for everyone in the store to hear, "we're talking mondo cool here."

"I just don't know if I trust him," Nancy whispered discreetly.

"What's trust got to do with it? It's a party." When Nancy didn't respond, Bess added, "And if you say no, I may have to confide in a certain Ned Nickerson back in River Heights that my best friend is falling for a billionaire."

"That's not true." This time it was Nancy's voice that could be heard across the store. "And that's blackmail."

Bess smiled and walked back before Nancy to join Welsch.

Welsch played his ace when Nancy came back. "Forsythe's appearance at your hotel this afternoon leads my people to believe that he, or others in Jericho's gang, or maybe even Jericho himself, may show up at the museum tonight. They believe that whatever scheme Jericho has, he'd want to get the lay of the land, or, in this case, the lay of the ship."

"That is a definite possibility," Nancy agreed.

Welsch smiled. "So it's your choice. Come for the atmosphere, or come for the intrigue. I know one of those has got to appeal to you."

"Why is a museum in Chicago giving this party?" Nancy questioned. Bess was about to explode if Nancy didn't say yes soon.

"Very simple. They're hoping to acquire some artifacts from the *Titanic*," Welsch answered. "I can pick you up at your hotel. Say, sevenish?" He paused, waiting for Nancy's answer.

Nancy turned to Bess, whose face she read loud and clear: Nancy Drew, I will never speak to you again if you don't say yes. Her own mind was saying: If anything happens there and you miss it, you will regret it.

"Seven forty-five," Nancy replied.

"Good. I'm glad we've gotten that settled. There is one more thing." Welsch reached into his inside jacket pocket and pulled out a slip of paper. "You're familiar with Stetson and Stevens?"

"Of course," Bess replied before Nancy could answer. "I've had a charge there for years."

"Well, you won't be needing it today. I've made arrangements with a personal shopper there, a Miss Erica, to assist you in finding what you'd like to wear tonight." He handed Bess the slip of paper with Miss Erica's name and extension number on it. "I don't imagine you came to Chicago with formal wear. They've been given instructions to put anything you wish on my account."

All smiles, Bess gave a little gasp.

"I think we've just accepted your kind offer," Nancy said, also smiling broadly. For Bess's benefit she added, "You'll have to trust us to exercise some restraint."

Welsch shook his head. "Restraint isn't something I'm interested in. Tonight is going to be a gala affair. My motto is, Don't go to a splash, be a splash."

"Now, that's a motto I could live by," Bess said.

"And if we decide our own clothes are good enough?" Nancy asked.

"Then by all means wear them," Welsch answered. "I'm merely affording you an alternative. I'd just like to have you there. If there's any trouble, please call me." He reached into his pocket again and gave Nancy his card.

"Oh, and one more thing," Welsch said. "May I leave my security team in place around you and Bess?"

Nancy didn't have to think about it, really. She certainly knew how to take care of herself, but it didn't hurt to have backup with the likes of Jericho and Forsythe around.

"Yes," she answered. "Thank you."

"My limousine will arrive at your hotel at seven forty-five. Until then . . ." Welsch nodded graciously and turned to go, but he stopped suddenly and snapped his fingers. Turning back to Nancy, he said, "I was serious about that blue dress."

He smiled his charming smile and walked out of the store.

"Wow!" Bess exclaimed. "I can't believe you're thinking about not going to Stetson and Stevens."

Nancy put Welsch's card in her purse and picked up the dress. She was going to buy it, but only because *she* liked it.

"Does any of this make sense to you, Bess? Why would Welsch show up and give us a Cinderella fantasy?"

"Who's worried about it making sense," Bess replied. "I'm just going to enjoy myself and get something really nice. Then I'm planning on having a blast at the party."

"Still, you have to wonder what his game is."

"Nancy," Bess admonished, "do you really believe a man as brilliant as Walter Welsch thinks he's going to sweep you off your feet by buying you a new party dress and picking you up in a limo? Get a grip. He's bound to have checked you out, just as you're checking him out. I think he's doing this because he can, and because he thinks you'd enjoy it. I know I'm going to."

"All my instincts are screaming that he's hiding something," Nancy protested.

"A guy who's made billions of dollars," Bess said, "is always going to have something to hide. It's the nature of the beast."

* * *

Joe threw an arm up to defend himself and deflected the kick so it landed against his shoulder. This caused his arm to go partially numb though. Knocked off balance, he stumbled for a moment before regaining his footing.

The man broke away and went racing up the hill.

The attacker's decision to run made absolutely no sense to Joe. The man had the advantage in size and strength, and he had a gun.

Joe grabbed hold of his walkie-talkie as he took off in pursuit of the spy. "Frank, I flushed him out, but he's making a break for it."

"I'll get the Jeep and drive it to the top of the hill," Frank replied. "Did you recognize him?"

"No." Joe said, saving his breath for running.

The man streaked through the trees, vaulting over brush effortlessly.

Joe pumped his arms and legs, digging into the terrain. He slowly began to gain on his man.

For the second time that day, Joe's lungs burned from lack of oxygen, but he concentrated on working through the pain. Summoning his will power, he began to sprint.

As they reached the crest, with the highway just yards ahead, Joe made a final effort and threw himself forward. His free hand lashed out and caught the man's foot.

The man struggled to free his trapped foot and maintain his balance. Unable to do either, he crashed to the ground. Joe fell with him. The man twisted and kicked back viciously.

Joe narrowly avoided finding out what it would be like to have his nose bashed in by rolling away and surging to his feet.

"Back off, Hardy!" the man shouted. "You're getting in way over your head." He reached for the pistol in his shoulder holster.

Moving swiftly, Joe brought his walkie-talkie down on the man's hand as the pistol cleared the leather. The weapon hit the dirt and the man roared.

Joe wondered how this guy knew his name and then realized that he'd be a pretty poor spy if he didn't know the names of the people he was spying on.

By the time those two thoughts had registered in Joe's brain, the man was on his feet and setting himself into a martial arts stance.

As Joe lined himself up to meet the upcoming attack, he noted a sedan idling across the highway. Joe quickly engaged his walkie-talkie. "Frank, this guy's not alone. There's a driver in an olive sedan up here."

Frank's reply got lost in the flurry of kicks Joe had to fend off, which he did successfully. Then he went on the offensive. He quickly stepped in and unloaded a short jab to the man's stomach.

The man's breath exploded over Joe's shoulder. The fight was over as the wounded spy stumbled off, trying to catch his breath.

The olive sedan was on the move. The driver, pistol in hand, was headed straight for Joe.

Suddenly Joe heard the sound of the Jeep

climbing up the incline fast. He looked from the driver in the approaching sedan to Frank in the Jeep. He realized that he wasn't in danger of being hit, but Frank was—and didn't know it.

Joe turned and started waving frantically at Frank. "Stop!" he yelled, but the word was lost in the roar of the engine as the Jeep nearly flew over the ridge. Joe leaped out of the way. He didn't want to watch, but he couldn't tear his eyes away. "Frank!"

The Jeep hit the shoulder of the highway with Frank already on top of the brake. Tires shrieking, the Jeep came to a shuddering stop at the same time as the sedan—inches separating them.

The sedan driver leveled his pistol at Frank. "Move the Jeep."

Joe scrambled over to the spy's pistol lying in the dirt, picked it up, and ran for the cover of a tree. "Frank," he yelled. "Reverse."

Frank hesitated for only a moment, then threw the Jeep in reverse and gunned it.

Joe took careful aim with his captured pistol and shot out the sedan's front tires. The front end of the vehicle sagged toward the ground as the tires deflated. He ducked back behind the tree, expecting return fire.

None came.

The driver of the sedan put his weapon away. "You shot out my tires. Truce, man, truce."

"Throw your gun out the window," Joe ordered.

"I'm not going to do it. I give you my word. You don't have anything to worry about from me."

"And we're going to believe you because you've got such an honest face?" Joe asked sarcastically.

"No, you're going to believe me," the man said, "because I'm with the Network."

Chapter

Thirteen

THE LAST WORD the driver spoke stopped Joe cold. He and Frank sometimes worked with and sometimes had to work their way around the Network. He had no fond feelings for the Network, but he did have a healthy respect. Joe flipped the safety on the pistol and stepped out from behind his cover.

"We can't tell you what we're working on here," Collins, the spy, said after Frank had joined Joe and introductions had been performed. "Or if we're working on anything at all."

Frank frowned. "Somehow I don't think you're here on vacation."

Agent Candless, the driver of the sedan, grinned. "He's got a point."

"What if I said that you two were interfering in a matter of national security?" Collins asked.

"By coming to Wedge Grove on vacation?" Joe replied. "Get real."

"What *are* you doing out here?" Candless asked.

"We're here on vacation," Frank replied. He looked over at Eric, who stood a way down the road, and waved. "That's our host."

Frank felt lousy for asking Eric to take a walk, but he knew they'd get nothing from the Network agents with him present.

"You came at a bad time," Collins stated.

"Convince us and we'll go home," Joe replied.

"We thought you guys might get the hint after last night," Collins said with a sneer.

"Those were Network people?" Joe demanded, taking a step toward the already injured man.

"Calm down," Candless said.

Joe stopped. "You didn't answer my question."

"Wasn't us," Candless protested. "We didn't know it was going down until it was over."

"You didn't know we were coming to the institute?" Frank asked.

Candless shook his head. "Believe it or not, we have more important things to work on."

"Then what were you doing spying on us today?" Joe asked.

"We do what we're told," Collins answered.

"Who *did* run us off the road?" Frank asked.

"We don't know," Candless said.

Frank knew the man was lying. Even if the

Network agents didn't know for sure, they at least had a good idea. But that didn't answer the question as to why they were following the brothers now.

A phone rang inside the sedan. Candless answered it, spoke briefly, then turned to Frank. "It's for you."

Frank took the handset as Joe crowded in close enough to hear. It was a call Frank had been expecting. "Hello, sir," he said.

"Good morning, Frank," the dry voice of the Gray Man greeted him. "I trust Joe is there as well."

"Yes," Joe answered.

"I'd appreciate it if you two would let my men simply go on their way," the Gray Man said. "If you tail them, they'll call me and I'll take them off their assignment. In fact, I may do that anyway."

"Because you have other agents already here in place?" Frank asked.

The Gray Man laughed dryly. "You know I play my cards closer to the vest than that."

"You could cut us in," Joe pointed out. "We're already here."

"No," the Gray Man said. "So what is it going to be? I can order those two agents to sit there until retirement."

Bess and Nancy sat in the back of the luxury limo and watched Walter Welsch talk over a phone headset while checking monitors lining the back of the seat. The views all came from security teams with small, portable cameras the billionaire had assigned inside the museum.

All the monitors reduced the banquet and party to a series of flat black-and-white images. Bess was in heaven, recognizing movie stars, athletes, and younger state politicians. She even knew some of the reporters covering the event.

Welsch finished his phone call only seconds after the limo glided to a stop at the bottom of the long stone steps leading up to the museum. He put his headset away and looked at Bess and Nancy.

"I am very sorry to have been so rude on our ride over here," Welsch said with a too-perfect tone of sincerity.

"I'm sure your call was important," Nancy replied so coldly that Bess shivered.

"That's okay, Walter," Bess said cheerfully. "You're a very busy businessman. You have to keep up your contacts all over the world, I imagine." She smiled sweetly at the billionaire, nothing but thrilled with the night.

"I hate to disappoint you, Bess," Welsch said, ducking his head a little, "but that wasn't a contact from some exotic foreign land offering me an oil well or two."

"Oh." He was right, Bess was disappointed. "Who was it?"

"Bess," Nancy chided.

"Your straightforwardness is refreshing, Bess," Welsch allowed. "I was speaking to my mother, who lives in Virginia. That's one contact whose calls I always take."

Before either of the girls had a chance to apologize, the chauffeur had the door open for them.

As the three stepped out, the anxious line of photographers and news reporters, who had been waiting for Welsch's arrival, burst into activity. Questions came flying through the air as camera flashes effectively blinded the threesome.

Bess wondered if the amount Nancy was hating this came close to amount that she was loving it. I bet she's still trying to find an ulterior motive for Walter's generosity, Bess thought.

Welsch glanced at his very well dressed companions. "Ready?"

Nancy nodded and graciously took the arm he offered her. Bess took his other arm with all the enthusiasm of a homecoming queen at a football game.

They were quite a handsome trio as they ascended the wide stairs to the museum. On either side of the stairway, colored lights shone on the museum's famous fountains from ancient Pompeii.

Nancy wore a long, burnt red gown with a fitted halter-neck bodice. Around her neck hung a sparkly necklace of red stones.

Bess's blond curly hair flowed like sunlight over her long black satin dress with seed pearls lining the generous neckline. The dress was complemented by a silvery see-through jacket, edged in black seed pearls.

Bess's feet were shod with a fine pair of pearly white satin heels. She and Nancy had almost had a fight in the shoe department because Nancy refused at first to get a new pair to go with her dress. She didn't want to take advantage of Welsch and his money.

"Does that mean I can buy two pairs?" Bess had jokingly asked her friend. Nancy started to blow up before she recognized that Bess was teasing. Nancy wound up with a pair of delicate gold sandals that accented her dark red dress beautifully.

Two lines of security men held back the reporters, forming a corridor for Welsch and his guests to pass through into the museum. They closed ranks behind the threesome as they walked into the brightly lit marble lobby.

"There," Welsch said with a grin, adjusting his jacket. "That wasn't too bad, was it?"

"That was great," Bess answered, gazing longingly back at the crowd now kept out by the uniformed police and the glass doors. "We get to do it again on the way out, right?"

Welsch chuckled. "If you like. Or we may manage to sneak out. This was just preparation for the crowds at our departure on the *Hampton* in New York. That's where all the crowds will be."

Welsch took their arms and guided them down a long hallway where they were greeted by a host and hostess looking as if they'd stepped from the pages of a fashion magazine.

As soon as Welsch stepped through the main doors, he was mobbed—this time by museum personnel, guests on the cruise, and reporters who'd been invited to cover the event.

Nancy's eyes followed the billionaire as he was carried off by the crowd. Bess looked around briefly, then her face lit in a smile. "Hey, look, Nan. There's Brook Richards."

Turning, Nancy spotted the young action-film star in a crowd of young women.

"Why is he here?" Bess wondered out loud.

"His upcoming picture is about an underwater marine salvage expert who gets caught between a Japanese crime syndicate and a crooked CIA agent," Nancy answered. "He probably got an invitation to help publicize the movie."

"Well, I'm going over to let him know I'm going to buy a ticket when the movie comes out," Bess declared. "Want an autograph?"

"No, thanks."

"You might regret it later," Bess warned.

"If I think I will," Nancy promised, "I'll be over."

Bess made a beeline for the movie star.

Nancy drifted by the heavily laden banquet

tables and accepted a glass of mineral water from one of the servers. She watched Walter Welsch make the rounds, impressed with the skill the man had in handling people. Even from a distance, she could hear that the billionaire spoke in four languages.

Sipping her water, Nancy made her way around the huge room, taking in all the displays that had been set up concerning the *Titanic* and its fateful maiden voyage.

An ice sculpture of the ship was the centerpiece of a cold seafood hors d'oeuvre table. Nancy imagined that more than one reporter would mention in the next day's papers that an ice sculpture of the most famous ship to sink after striking an iceberg was perhaps not in the best of taste.

Paintings, drawings, and etchings of the *Titanic* adorned the walls. Nancy found the images far more disturbing and haunting than the ice sculpture.

Abruptly, her attention was captured by the steamrolling approach of a long-limbed woman with oval-shaped glasses and a tan, complete with windburn. She wore a simple black dress that created an aura of power and elegance.

A handful of men and women called out to her, trying, it seemed, to get her to turn around and abandon whatever quest she was on. The woman didn't pause but cut straight through the crowd toward Walter Welsch. She didn't stop until she was eye to eye with the billionaire.

"Ladies and gentlemen," Welsch said with aplomb and a smile, "may I introduce Libby McCarthy."

Nancy felt the electricity between the two from across the room.

Libby spoke softly, so her voice didn't carry to Nancy's ears. From the woman's body language, however, Nancy understood that she was not happy, nor was she weak.

Nancy moved closer.

"So don't try to win me over with your charm," Libby was saying, "because I've been there and done that. I never believed in anyone more fully than you, Walter, nor have I ever been betrayed more fully."

"Libby," Welsch said in a strained voice, "I wish I knew what to say."

Nancy was unimpressed with his comeback.

"There is nothing to say," Libby countered. Her face trembled for a moment and bright tears shone unshed in her green eyes. "I can't even believe I'm here trying to say it. I came here to drum up support against raising the *Titanic*."

"Let's go somewhere," Welsch said, reaching for her. "We can talk."

"No. It's not about talk anymore," the woman said, pushing his arm away. "It's about actions. And if you stay on this course, you're making the biggest mistake of your life." She turned abruptly and half ran, half walked away. She was gone as abruptly as she had appeared.

"The second biggest mistake," Welsch said quietly as he watched her go.

Nancy's mind rattled in frustration. Did he mean that the woman was the second biggest mistake of his life or that letting her go was?

"Oh, wow," Bess said over Nancy's shoulder. "Now, *that* was a scene." Bess had appeared behind her without warning.

"Was it ever," Nancy said in agreement, watching to see how the billionaire would recover.

Welsch turned back to the group of people surrounding him, and their animated discussion continued as if it hadn't been interrupted.

A few minutes later Welsch broke away and rejoined Nancy and Bess. "How have you ladies been?" he asked.

"Probably doing much better than you," Bess stated bluntly.

Welsch was caught off guard but only for a moment. "Yes, well, things don't always go as one would like. Even for me. I guess it only proves I'm human, despite what some people may think."

Part of Nancy silently commiserated with the man over the disagreement he'd had with the woman. It was obvious she meant something to him, just as it was obvious that he meant something to her.

But another part of Nancy's mind demanded

to know the full story on Walter Welsch. How had he betrayed the woman, and over what?

Abruptly, her attention was drawn to a familiar face cruising one of the banquet tables. Her memory jogged a name into place. She took Welsch's arm and leaned toward him. "Hugo Danby just made the party," she said.

Welsch took a sip of his mineral water. "You're sure?"

"Yes," Nancy said. "He's originally from France, where he worked the black market trade. Danby was with Jericho almost from the start of his rogue days."

Welsch put his glass down on a nearby table. "Let's walk over to him, but be careful. I don't want to spook him. Bess, please excuse us."

Still holding Welsch's arm, Nancy chatted lightly about the expected weather for the cruise as she did as he had asked. The international thief didn't seem to notice them.

"Him?" Welsch pointed his chin imperceptibly at Danby.

The thief was a tall, thin, pale man. He wore all black, which suited him as naturally as if he were a panther. He smiled nicely, talking with a young woman at his side.

Without changing her expression or tone of voice, Nancy replied, "Yes."

Welsch held a finger to one ear. "Do you have the man in sight?"

It was only then that Nancy was aware of the small earplug in the billionaire's ear.

"Then take him," Welsch instructed.

Moving like a well-oiled team, four men stepped from the ranks of the banquet attendees. They approached Danby from all sides, giving the man no chance to escape. With a minimum of disturbance they hustled him toward Welsch and Nancy.

"He's wanted on a number of outstanding charges," Welsch said to Nancy, "so an arrest should stick."

Welsch stepped forward, towering over the thief. "Hugo Danby," he said.

"I'm afraid you've got the wrong man," the man replied.

"I don't think so," Welsch said. He nodded at his security staff and they pulled Danby off through the crowd.

Welsch let out a deep breath. "Okay. That confirms that Jericho and his people are players in my *Titanic* operation. Obviously Jericho sent that man here to spy."

"I'd say so, but what could they have been hoping to learn?" Nancy wondered out loud.

Welsch swept his gaze over the crowd. "Some of the richest people in the Chicago area are here tonight, and many will be aboard the *Hampton.* Maybe Jericho just wanted to be able to make a hit list. We have never published a passenger list. Care to take a walk around the hall? Maybe we'll get lucky again."

Nancy and Welsch strolled casually among the guests. Here and there, the billionaire greeted a guest, while Nancy mentally filed impressions.

Welsch certainly didn't have all his cards on the table. Who was Libby McCarthy? Why were Amos Jericho and his band of thieves interested in the cruise? Nancy wondered again if perhaps Walter Welsch was working *with* Jericho.

Chapter

Fourteen

In THE END, Joe knew there was no real choice, no matter how unfair he considered the situation. After the phone call with the Gray Man ended, Joe grumpily got behind the wheel of the Jeep and started the engine.

Frank raided the cooler and left sandwiches and soft drinks with the Network agents. They'd be there awhile waiting for a garage to send someone out to fix their two flat tires.

"That," Joe declared when Frank clambered aboard the Jeep, "was a waste of goodwill." He pulled the Jeep onto the highway.

"Maybe," Frank agreed. "But I couldn't see leaving them stranded without supplies."

"I could."

"Joe," Eric said from the passenger seat, "I

144

think you've gotten even meaner than I remember."

"It's those guys," Joe complained. "I get the feeling one hand doesn't know what the other is doing."

"Or exactly how many hands are involved," Frank put in.

"Things certainly haven't changed for the two of you," Eric said. "Always in something up to your eyeballs."

Joe grinned at his friend, his anger already dissipating. It was good to think of the embarrassment they'd provided the two Network agents who'd thought they could spy on them without getting caught. "And if we're lucky, things will *never* change." He looked back at Frank in the rear of the Jeep. "What did you find down the incline?"

"An added twist to the mystery," Frank replied. He pushed his fist forward, and Joe could see the brass glinting through the plastic sandwich bag dangling between his fingers. "Tell me what you see."

Joe glanced at the short rifle cartridges in the bag, noticing immediately the curiously crinkled openings, where the explosions had erupted. "Those guys last night were shooting blanks!"

"Definitely not all of those shots were blanks," Frank replied, examining the plastic bag of spent cartridges again. The Hardys and Eric had retreated to Frank's room at the institute after snagging something to snack on from the kitchen.

"We've got a couple of bullet holes in the van to prove that."

"It doesn't make sense," Eric said. "From what you told me, those guys came on like gangbusters. If they were only trying to scare you, they were taking a big chance using live ammunition."

"They were pros," Frank reminded him. "They knew exactly what they were doing."

"In a way," Joe said, "it makes even less sense for those guys to try to scare us than to hurt us."

Frank nodded in agreement. "We thought they were there investigating us, but they already knew all about us. They knew our names, they knew when we would be arriving at the institute, and they knew what we were driving."

"Do you think they were trying to send you a message?" Eric asked.

"What?" Joe asked. "To stay away? If they knew us as well as we think, they'd have known that their tactics would have failed. A midnight attack is just the sort of thing that piques my interest."

"Maybe we're looking at this from the wrong end," Frank suggested. "If they really wanted us to stay away, they'd have hurt us. But they didn't, so we think the attack is some kind of message."

"Where are you going with this, Frank?" Joe opened his hands in a gesture of "What gives?"

Frank had grown almost immune to Joe's

impatience. He let it pass, but moved on to the point. "What if the message wasn't for us? What if we were just the messengers?"

"Oh, wow," Joe said. Frank could just about see his brain whirring.

"Let's assume for a moment that Libby Mc-Carthy is correct and Walter Welsch really is behind the sabotage problems at the institute," Frank continued. "Including blowing up the motor sailer. Why would he bother with us?"

"Dad," Joe said. "Welsch might be afraid that we'd get Dad interested in what's going on at the institute. Then Dad might come up here and sort it out."

"I don't think it's Dad," Frank said. "Too much of a risk. If we'd gotten hurt, Dad would have been up here in a minute and they'd be in prison by now."

"Point," Joe said in agreement.

"But back up. You said something important. Just what *is* going on at the institute?" Frank asked. "Do you believe someone like Walter Welsch would be worried about Libby giving the media a closer look at the *Titanic* recovery?"

Joe shook his head. "No way. Sure, Welsch might be making money off the television deals, but what's a few million to someone like him? And if I was Welsch, I wouldn't have blown up a motor sailer if I wanted to cut down on the competition. I would have taken out the *Manta* once and for all. That way Libby would have no footage of the *Titanic* either to sell or give away."

"Whoa," Eric said suddenly. "You think the attack was designed to scare off Libby McCarthy?" He snorted and shook his head. "Wrong! Way wrong! Libby doesn't budge and she doesn't bend unless she wants to. She's about as likely to give in to scare tactics as you guys."

"The explosion this morning seemed to shake her up," Joe observed. "Maybe the attack and the explosion were meant to be a one-two punch. Just keep piling on the trouble until she breaks."

"It didn't happen, though," Eric argued. "She's more determined than ever that the demonstration will be a success."

"You're right," Frank said, shaking his head. "Where does that leave us?"

"What about those two goons this afternoon?" Joe asked. "Why is the agency on our tail?"

"What agency?" Eric asked.

Joe looked at Frank with guilty embarrassment. Frank realized that Joe hadn't mentioned the Network in front of Eric until that very moment. Eric was a good friend, and brilliant. Frank wished he could let him in on the whole story because he could be a lot of help.

"We can't tell you," Frank said plainly.

"Otherwise we'd have to kill you," Joe cracked.

"Terrific," Eric grumbled. "But I'm right that this is a government agency involved in covert matters."

"You make it sound like something out of a comic book," Joe stated.

"Pardon me," Eric replied. "I don't get out to do much *real* detective work."

An uncomfortable silence settled around the friends. Frank made a choice.

"Yes," he said, though he knew he could be taking a risk just admitting that much. "It's a government agency."

"Which shall remain nameless. Cool. It makes me feel all tingly just knowing that much." Eric grinned at the brothers, who took his teasing well. "Seriously," he continued, "Libby has worked with some of the more secret agencies in the past on salvage operations, and Norman Lowell used to be affiliated with the CIA."

"Now we're cooking," Frank said. "What are the chances that the agency's presence here, now, has something to do with Libby or Lowell?"

Eric summed up his doubt in one word. "Cold. Libby works strictly within the institute's guidelines. Even her demonstration against raising the *Titanic* has been okayed by the board. And Lowell hasn't been with the CIA in two years or more. I've seen his résumé—what there is of it. Looking at all the holes in it, you get the impression that the guy has been in a lot of hot spots."

"Dead end, there," Joe pointed out. "I have a basic question. Why would the government be interested in an ocean liner that sank nearly ninety years ago?"

Chapter

Fifteen

JOE SPED ACROSS the sand, following the arc of the volleyball, still amazed that Eric had returned his spike.

"It's yours, Hardy!" Mandy yelled. She ran with him for backup. "Set!"

Joe tracked Mandy's position out of the corner of his eye. The ball was coming in too low to return while standing, so Joe took a flying dive at it. He barely got his hands under the ball, digging it up only inches above the sand before he bellyflopped onto the beach.

The ball arced high, only a few degrees off the perfect rebound.

"Get up! Get up!" Mandy yelled. "You've got to return it!" She cupped her hands before her, driving the ball off her wrists into the air.

Joe was not used to playing volleyball in the

sand. Every one of his muscles was crying out from the exertion. He wasn't interested only in the game. This was his first chance to really impress Mandy. He leaped up from the sand and, hunkering down to receive Mandy's set, he uncoiled and sprang up after the ball. He pumped an open hand at it, faking a drive.

Eric and the player to his right ran to the place Joe had aimed. While they were out of position, Joe spiked the ball into the hole they'd left behind.

"Game!" Mandy said shrilly.

Joe dropped to his knees, exhausted, and gazed up at Mandy, hoping for some sign of approval, a high-five at least.

Instead, Mandy walked over to the sidelines and picked up a couple of towels, her sunglasses, and her bottle of water. She tossed Joe a towel and slid her sunglasses on.

"Good game, Hardy," she said as she turned and walked away.

"Yeah, you, too," Joe said to her retreating figure.

"She really drives you, doesn't she?" Eric asked, coming over to join Joe. "Tells you exactly where she expects you to be during a game. I've never seen anyone more addicted to winning. Why, even you pale in comparison."

"I thought if we won a game together, she might consider lunch some time." Joe breathed through his mouth.

"Not Mandy," Oliver said. He'd been sitting on the sidelines, watching the game.

"Has she got somebody?" Joe asked.

"If she does," her brother answered, "she's keeping him to herself. Mandy likes her own company best."

Joe watched as Mandy walked across the parking lot and slid behind the wheel of a red Corvette.

"She has expensive tastes as well," Eric chimed in. "Buddy, face it. You just don't have the budget for her. Even if you got her to give you a second glance."

"Yeah, yeah, yeah." Joe watched the sports car. "So tell me, Oliver, what's the inside scoop on your sister?"

"You got me," Oliver replied. "My twin was always the quiet one when we were growing up. She entered the Air Force after college. Mandy was good at what she did, and she was involved in a number of need-to-know operations. I didn't see her much again until her hitch was over and we hooked up here at Wedge Grove a few months ago."

Eric smiled. "I think Joe would definitely like to hook up with her here, too."

Oliver laughed, and Joe just shook his head. Mandy's aloofness was a definite attraction.

The two days since the sinking of the motor sailer had been quiet around the institute, though tense. Between swimming and sailing with Frank and Eric, Joe had tried to get to know

Mandy better, but she'd rejected his attempts at every turn.

Casting a wistful glance at the parking lot, Joe saw Frank walking toward them carrying a bottle of water.

"How was your luck today?" Frank asked Joe.

"What luck?" Joe mumbled.

Frank let out an exaggerated groan. "He gets so grumpy when he loses at volleyball."

Eric and Oliver snorted their laughter, much to Frank's confusion.

"Oh, he won the game," Eric explained. "But he didn't win over Mandy."

"Oh, I see," Frank said. "That makes him even grumpier." He bent toward Joe's ear and whispered. "No time for games, now, brother. We just got a call from the Gray Man. He's offering us a job. Want to call him back and tell him we're interested?"

Frank and Joe went to Frank's room to return the Gray Man's call.

"Care to do the honors?" Frank asked, holding the phone out to his brother.

"All yours," Joe replied. "After our little adventure with the Network the other day, I'm afraid I might say something you'd regret."

"It's a good thing one of us is a diplomat," Frank said, and sat on his bed.

"And I'm glad it's you."

While Frank dialed and waited for the connection, Joe stared out the window overlooking the institute's marina.

Every ship that could be freed up for the *Titanic* demonstration was berthed there, with crews scurrying over the decks like ants, getting ready. Tomorrow morning, at first light, they'd take to the ocean on an intercept course with Welsch's liner, the *Hampton*. Libby had timed the trip so that the institute's boats would reach the *Titanic*'s recovery site at approximately the same time as the cruise liner. The trip would take the better part of four days, and Frank and Joe hoped to be there.

"Hello," the Gray Man answered.

The Gray Man always answered his own phone because no one knew the number except those he wanted to talk to.

"We're interested," Frank said.

"Good," the Gray Man responded.

"What's the gig?" Joe demanded of Frank, who frowned and signaled Joe to shut up.

"I want you to go aboard the *Hampton,*" the Gray Man continued. "I'm sure you know of the ship."

"Yes," Frank said. "How would you suggest we get on board?"

"On board where?" Joe asked.

Frank gave his brother a menacing look.

"You'll find you've been invited," the Gray Man answered. "They'll be expecting you to arrive by helicopter, which has been arranged. Your cover is as reporters for your local Bayport paper. Your identification papers will be in the helicopter."

"What is it you want us to report on?" Frank asked.

"Report? What? Where?" Joe took three steps across the room, looking as if he were ready to tear the phone out of Frank's hand.

Frank casually stuck his foot out and caught Joe's ankle, which sent Joe to the floor. Frank stood up and glared at his brother while listening intently. For good measure, he rested his foot on Joe's back.

"Frank? Is there some trouble there? I heard something at your end," the Gray Man questioned.

"Fine, sir. Everything's fine," Frank said. "Joe just stumbled. He's fine." Frank applied a little more pressure to Joe's back as insurance.

"All right. I want you to identify a passenger aboard the *Hampton* if you can," the Gray Man continued.

"Who?" Frank asked.

"Who?" echoed Joe.

"I don't know what name he's traveling under," the Gray Man replied, "or I'd already have him in custody. His real name is Adnan Ibrahim. He was a terrorist until his retirement, when he began dealing in arms. Large weaponry. Lately, he's been brokering for the Libyans. There's a computer aboard the helicopter. You'll find a file on him in its E-mail. Once you and Joe have read it through and studied the pictures, destroy the file."

Joe heaved Frank's foot off his back and stood

up next to him. Frank shot him a look that meant, "Behave," and angled the phone so they both could listen.

"Why don't you send one of your own people?" Frank asked, well aware of how little patience the Gray Man had with questions.

"I already have agents in place aboard the *Hampton,*" the Gray Man said. "The problem is, Ibrahim is familiar with them. My sources informed me that Ibrahim would not be brokering the deal himself. If I'd known that wasn't true, I would have planned earlier to send in others, such as yourselves."

Frank was surprised to hear of that kind of misinformation at the Gray Man's level—whatever that level was. "What deal is he brokering?" he asked.

"I'm afraid that's classified," the Gray Man replied.

"You're asking us to stick out our necks here," Joe suddenly interrupted, grabbing the phone from Frank. "I think we need to know."

"Hello, Joe. You don't need to know," the Gray Man said simply.

"Then maybe we don't need to sign on for this," Joe shot back. Frank tried to take the phone back but lost the struggle.

The Gray Man's voice remained neutral. "It's your call. If you say no, I'll go elsewhere. You're my first choice, but by no means the only choice."

Frank stood in front of Joe, his face inches from his brother's. Joe gave him the phone.

"Okay," Frank said. "We'll take it. When do we leave?"

"Now," the Gray Man answered.

In the distance, Frank heard helicopter rotors beating, growing nearer. The phone clicked dead in his hand.

It seemed as if all the world had turned out to see the *Hampton* sail from New York harbor. Given the size of the international press corps present, Nancy thought that estimate might not be exaggerated.

"Nancy, can you believe we're here for this," Bess said excitedly. "Actually, just being in New York again is almost thrilling enough."

After having flown in from Chicago the night before, they now stood together at the railing of the *Hampton* as colorful confetti and streamers spilled down from the ship's decks. Crowds thronged the docks, as well as the *Hampton*'s decks.

"It's a rush, isn't it?" Nancy agreed. The sun felt good against her skin, and the breeze blowing in off the harbor swirled around her.

News helicopters hung in the sky like predatory birds. Huge signs with Bon Voyage, *Hampton* on them adorned the sides of nearby buildings.

It was, in Nancy's opinion, a great send-off

from the city. Just then the final horn sounded, and amid even greater cheering the *Hampton* eased away from its dock. Nancy had sailed a few times, but she never lost the thrill of those initial seconds when a ship gets under way.

"Tell me what you think."

Nancy Drew turned around and found Walter Welsch standing behind her. "It's incredible," she replied honestly as the ship moved out into the harbor toward the Statue of Liberty.

The billionaire grinned. He was dressed in a brilliant white suit more appropriate for a leisure cruise in the Caribbean than a working trip on the frigid Atlantic Ocean. "I'm glad you think so. I'd have hated to see this floating party fall flat on its face."

"It's so elegant," Nancy went on. "I imagine the *Titanic* itself must have felt this luxurious."

"More so. They didn't have *that* crowd underfoot. Welsch nodded his head toward the pockets of media personnel who were staking out their territory for observing the raising of the *Titanic* in four more days. Meanwhile, TV talk show hosts were busy interviewing anyone who would stop to talk to them.

"But they're giving you all the publicity you could wish for," Nancy reminded him.

"True," he replied with a fond look at her, "though I'd prefer to be a guest at this party than the host. I'll have to make sure to keep you nearby to remind me of my duties."

Nancy laughed. She felt a little self-conscious about all the attention Welsch had continued to give her since the night of the party in Chicago. She tried deflecting the topic of conversation away from herself. "Bess, here, doesn't mind the cameras, do you?" Nancy turned to discover her best friend was gone.

As if on cue, however, Bess walked out of one of lounges with a network anchor, followed by a camera crew with film rolling.

"See what I mean?" Nancy asked.

"I'm pleased that Bess is enjoying herself. That's a rare talent," Welsch observed. "Tell me, Nancy, are you glad you accepted my invitation?"

Very," Nancy answered. "It's a once-in-a-lifetime chance."

"That it is." Welsch leaned against the railing and gazed down into the water. Behind him, just a few yards away, a third bodyguard joined the two who had been standing by since Welsch and Nancy had started talking. They looked just like the secret service who guard the president of the United States, right down to their dark glasses and knife-edge pressed pants and jackets.

"You know," Nancy mused, "I've read a number of articles about you."

"Ah, you must have trouble sleeping," Welsch joked. "There are a lot of them out there. Do me a favor and try to believe the good ones."

"That's not so hard," Nancy said, suddenly

realizing that she would have to work harder not to fall for his charm—at least until she'd discovered whether he was connected with Carter's death or not.

If only he hadn't put in such a quick appearance at the Chicago Police Department the night Carter had been killed. Then, Nancy thought, I'd have no trouble believing he was one of the good guys.

"None of those articles explains your fascination with the *Titanic*," Nancy prompted him.

"Maybe that's because I can't explain it myself," the billionaire said with a boyish grin. "When I was a kid, I read a lot—still do—but then you couldn't have gotten me within ten feet of a history book.

"I also watched a lot of television. One night, I saw a documentary on the *Titanic,* and I couldn't get enough of it. Suddenly I was reading every history book that mentioned it.

"Then I got hooked on World War I, which started just two years after the *Titanic* sank, then World War II, and books about ships and sunken treasures. One thing led to another, and here we are."

"There's a lot of speculation about what sent the *Titanic* to the bottom of the ocean," Nancy said. "What do you think sank her?"

"There are at least two different ways to answer that question," Welsch pointed out. "I'd say that obviously it was the iceberg that they hit that did in the ship, but it was the disastrous lack of attention to detail and a disrespect for nature that turned the *Titanic* into a tragedy. Where were the lifeboats? Where were the life preservers? Why were they going so fast?

"Have you seen the holographic show I arranged down in the Tesla Lounge on deck A?" Welsch asked, not giving Nancy a chance to respond to his views on the sinking of the *Titanic."*

"I couldn't get in," Nancy explained. "There must have been about a hundred people in the room when I tried."

"Let me take you there now. I'll clear the lounge if there are too many people and give you a private showing," Welsch declared.

"Sure," Nancy said. She looked around briefly to see if Bess was still nearby, but her friend had disappeared along with the TV men. Nancy sighed. Bess was going to be awfully jealous when she found out she'd missed a chance to be squired around by the billionaire again.

Nancy took Welsch's arm and tried not to notice how attractive he was.

Joe took one last look at Adnan Ibrahim's thin, harsh features on the computer monitor before deleting the file. He could do no better memorizing the man's face, and besides, the file had emphasized that Ibrahim was a master of disguise.

Frank sat across from Joe in the cargo area of the Bell 222 helicopter, peering out the window at the Atlantic Ocean below. Like Joe, he wore jeans, dress boots, and a sport coat. It was casual attire for someone dropping in from the sky to invade the most popular event of the decade, but neither of them had packed for business.

"Captain Taft, do you see the *Hampton?*" Joe asked the pilot over the radio link-up on the helicopter.

"We're banking in for descent now," crackled a voice through the headset into Joe's ear. "We've been cleared for boarding."

"Good." Joe was anxious to get started. Spending hours onboard an uncomfortable helicopter above the Atlantic Ocean wasn't his idea of a vacation.

They'd stayed over in New York the night before, in a less than luxurious hotel, which the Gray Man had arranged. On the highly unlikely chance that their man might appear, they had watched the launch of the *Hampton* on the television news shows. The brothers had gotten a good look at the famous billionaire Walter Welsch.

The helicopter started a steep descent, causing Joe's stomach to twist. In spite of his vague nausea, he gazed through the window behind him for a sight of the *Hampton*. He watched as the surface of the Atlantic Ocean came closer and closer and the cruise liner suddenly swelled into view. Yellow tape roped off the helicopter pad where a few crew members were waiting. Joe was ready.

A scaled-down, holographic *Titanic* sailed through a gap in the thick clouds of charcoal-gray fog at the front of the Tesla Lounge. Suddenly the detail was so sharp that Nancy could read the ocean liner's name on her prow. Cabin lights reflected the mist shrouding the hull of the ship.

"I have never seen anything like this!" Nancy exclaimed in awe. "I'd heard the re-enactment was carefully crafted, but I didn't expect anything like this." She stood near the front of the considerable crowd.

Walter Welsch beamed with pride. "You've heard of Magik Bytes?"

Nancy nodded. "Anyone who reads the credits at the end of movies these days knows about their awesome special effects. I also read the business section of the paper, so I know you own some of the company."

"Fifty-one percent, to be exact. Their top designers and programmers created this," Welsch explained. "It's amazing what you can do with creativity when you throw money at it."

Nancy looked at him to try to see how he meant that. Was he boasting or being cynical? She couldn't tell. He was almost as much of a mystery as why Jericho killed Carter.

Nancy wasn't the only one marveling at the three-dimensional laser light show, complete with surround sound. The lounge buzzed with the oohs and aahs people usually reserved for fireworks.

She'd seen re-creations of the *Titanic*'s sinking several times on film and television screens, but none of them came close to this breathtaking display. Despite its Lilliputian scale, Nancy felt as if she were watching the actual event.

The chatter in the room stilled and died, and Nancy felt cold dread seep into her bones as the shifting fog revealed the first of the virtual-reality icebergs. Time seemed to stand still as she listened to the sound of freezing waves slap the ship's sides.

Suddenly the mesmerizing lullaby was shattered by the terrifying noise of ice tearing into a ship's hull.

Chapter

Sixteen

FOR ONE CRAZY MOMENT, Nancy felt the fear that the *Titanic* passengers and crew must have experienced that fateful night on April 14, 1912.

A few seconds later the computer-generated image of the *Titanic* lit up as small, programmed figures scattered across the ocean liner's decks. The ship ground to a halt, but Nancy couldn't see where the iceberg had hit. Was it on the other side of the ship?

Nancy quickly took a few steps so she could see the opposite side of the display. There were icebergs on both sides, but none seemed to have come into contact with the *Titanic*. She looked questioningly at Welsch, who had followed her.

"Mysterious, isn't it, Nancy?" he asked in a low, vaguely sinister voice.

The sound system was exploding with noise:

passengers screaming, running feet, alarms, shouted orders, and the awful shriek of tearing metal.

Nancy recalled what she had learned in history class about the accident. No one had seen the iceberg that night. It hadn't been for lack of looking that the iceberg escaped notice. Only one tenth of any iceberg is visible above the water, and the part of the iceberg that tore into the *Titanic* was completely submerged. The tip of the iceberg appeared beside the ship, seemingly harmless. No one saw the collision, but everyone aboard must have heard it and felt the so-called unsinkable *Titanic* shudder.

The lights in the Tesla Lounge grew bright as the nighttime scene before Nancy faded away. She found herself breathing more steadily once the ship retreated back into history.

"Are you all right?" Welsch asked.

"It's a bit much," Nancy replied honestly. "It's one thing to read about the sinking or watch animated footage of it, but it's another to go through it like this."

"The program is edited down, but it is disquieting," Welsch said. "I wanted it to be that way."

Nancy studied the man's face. Perhaps he was as cold-blooded as some people thought. "I think I've had enough," she said.

"I understand. May I walk you back to the outer deck?"

Nancy nodded. Welsch waved at his security

staff and the human tide before them was pushed aside.

They were out on the main deck again in minutes. Grateful for the lingering sunshine, Nancy took long, deep breaths, surprised at the intensity of her reaction to the computer program.

"Sorry," she said.

"It's quite all right." Welsch smiled. "I'm actually quite flattered. The night we met, you seemed more together than you do now and you'd been under gunfire. I consider your reaction a compliment."

They stood for a moment silently staring ahead into nothing but mile after mile of ocean.

"Contrary to popular opinion," Welsch continued, "raising the *Titanic* isn't an expensive whim. I guess I just want to know that I did something worthwhile in my life, you know?" He laughed. "I probably sound very presumptuous."

"Not necessarily," Nancy replied. That's the scary part, she thought. "I think it depends on how you feel about disturbing the site. Some people feel very strongly that what you're doing is as sacrilegious as grave robbing."

Welsch shook his head. "Don't I know it."

He was stopped from saying more as one of his security men stepped forward. He had one hand cupped over the transceiver in his ear, and he spoke rapidly to Welsch, pitching his voice so Nancy couldn't hear.

Without a word, Welsch stepped to a television monitor inside the nearest lounge.

Nancy followed, curious to see what had dragged him away so abruptly. A woman occupied most of the screen. She stood in front of a large sailboat mast, and the motion of the camera suggested that her ship was under way.

"I don't have the proof I once had," the woman was saying, "but I know that a man in Walter Welsch's employ broke into the Wedge Grove Oceanography Institute and tried to sabotage our efforts to be here today."

The camera panned over to a news anchor who stood unsteadily beside the woman.

"So," the anchor began her wrap up, "even as Walter Welsch's quest to raise the *Titanic* from her watery grave is under way, we discover another twist to the story. Perhaps in his zeal to achieve what seems like a fantastic feat to most onlookers, Welsch is guilty of stepping on the dreams and beliefs of others. If Dr. McCarthy is correct in her convictions, Walter Welsch has a lot to answer for."

"Oh, Libby," Welsch groaned in a voice so low that Nancy felt she had not meant to hear it, "you're so wrong."

"Okay, so exactly how do you plan to find someone who can look like anyone he wants to?" Joe asked.

Frank grinned. Walter Welsch's security people had cleared them for free run of the ship nearly an hour ago. They'd taken a quick tour of the *Hampton* before settling in one of the main lounges to plan their strategy.

"Consider the situation," Frank said. "Not only does Ibrahim have to make sure he's not recognized, he's also got to be protected. Even if he changes his features, what would he keep around him that probably won't change?"

Joe sipped his soft drink and studied the crowd in the lounge again. A band was playing tunes from the sixties and a good number of people were out on the dance floor.

"His lucky socks," Joe finally said in frustration. "Come on, Frank, I'm wondering if we should even be here. Maybe the Gray Man lured us away from the institute's demonstration so he can take them out."

"You're getting paranoid," Frank replied.

"Try it for a while and see what you think," Joe said.

Out of the corner of his eye, Frank detected something—he wasn't sure whether it was a movement, a color, or a shape—that caught his attention. Was it Ibrahim? Searching the crowd, he lit upon a familiar figure. "Hey, isn't that Bess Marvin?"

All decked out in a sailor suit, Bess was dancing with a ship's officer dressed in a white uniform. She was all smiles.

Joe turned to look. "You're right. That's her. I wonder what she's doing here."

"Let me guess," Frank said. "We're on a ship

in the Atlantic on its way to observe the *Titanic* being raised. I've got it! She's probably here to see the *Titanic* being raised."

"Don't be hasty, Frank," Joe said. "I think I'd investigate before jumping to a conclusion like that."

Frank shook his head. His brother's humor was worse than his own.

"In case you happen to remember my question, I think the answer is his bodyguards," Frank said as Joe got up from the table.

Joe stared at him blankly. Sparks tended to flash between him and Bess Marvin, and even though neither of them seemed inclined to pursue the matter, Joe tended to be distracted whenever she was near.

"His bodyguards," Frank repeated. "Chances are Ibrahim would bring along the two who have been with him since his terrorist days. Remember? From the E-mail the Gray Man sent us? They aren't likely to be able to disguise themselves as well as their boss."

"Right," Joe said as he started off toward the dance floor. "I won't forget."

Frank watched with amusement as Joe cut in on Bess's dance partner effortlessly. With the two of them occupied, he decided to scope out the ship some more.

He spent the next hour casing the decks for Ibrahim's bodyguards while keeping an eye out for Nancy Drew. It wasn't usual for Bess to appear unless Nancy was leading the way. Frank didn't mind the idea of seeing his feisty friend again in the least.

Taking his time, Frank finally worked his way around the ship to the outdoor pool area. His blood stirred with excitement when he found one of Ibrahim's bodyguards seated at the bar just behind the diving board.

The second bodyguard sat in a chaise longue dressed in a heavy jacket, which was too hot but could easily hide a good-size gun.

Frank checked out the guests next, trying to identify the arms dealer. He had the field narrowed to four possibles when the bodyguards got up and followed a fifth—a stooped old man— out of the area.

Hanging back, Frank followed the three to a suite on the top deck. Before they disappeared through the door, Frank got a pretty good look at Ibrahim. He could scarcely believe what he saw. The pictures he had seen showed a tall, strong fighter. This man was seventy at least, and not a terribly healthy seventy.

Frank congratulated himself. This was easier than I had expected, he thought. Maybe too easy. He recalled what Joe had said about the Gray Man's just using this as a ruse to get them away from the Wedge Grove demonstration.

One phone call would settle whether the Gray Man would stand behind his promise to get them back to the Wedge Grove ships. He'd make that call as soon as he retrieved Joe.

As he threaded his way along a narrow passageway, however, he was diverted from his plans.

Nancy strode through the mazelike passageways and down companionways toward the cabin she and Bess were sharing. Bess has a nose for men, she thought. She'll be able to help me work out whether Walter Welsch is a murdering criminal or not.

Nancy felt more sympathy with Welsch than she would have thought possible. Still, he had been in Chicago the night Carter was killed. What if the billionaire had arranged the cyberthief's death to publicize the *Titanic* cruise? It wasn't that farfetched, and, whatever Welsch said, publicity was key to his empire.

The ringing sound of footsteps on the metal companionway beside Nancy barely touched her consciousness, but when the footsteps stopped, she turned toward the spot where the sound had been and found herself staring right into Chauncey Forsythe's cold gray eyes.

"Couldn't stay out of it, could you, love?" he asked in a hoarse whisper.

Nancy started to back away, looking up and down the companionway for help. No one was there.

"You followed me," Nancy said.

Forsythe nodded and opened his jacket, revealing a compact silver-colored pistol. "You've made quite a good friend in Mr. Walter Welsch, I see." He made a point of glancing up and down the stairs too. "As you can see, we are not likely to be disturbed here. However, should you choose to involve anyone else, I shan't be afraid to use this on them, too. Now, *you* will follow *me.*"

Nancy quickly considered her options and chose stalling for time. "What do you want?" she asked.

"To continue our little chat," the man replied. "In your cabin. See, I've looked all over this tub and I've not found hide nor hair of Amos Jericho."

"I told you what I knew in Chicago," Nancy declared. "I haven't learned anything more since then."

"That may be so, love, but I didn't come all this way to be played the fool. I want to know where Jericho is. If you don't know, you will find out for me."

Nancy prepared to execute her second option. If she could get in the first blow, maybe she could prevent him from drawing his pistol.

"Where's your little friend?" Forsythe was asking, when suddenly a shadow moved away from the corner toward him.

"Her dance card is pretty full," a deep voice declared. It was a voice that Nancy knew instantly. "But I'm free. Shall we dance?"

Forsythe reached for his weapon, but Frank moved with greater speed, bringing a round-house kick up and into Forsythe's chest. Forsythe went flying back against the wall. Before he could recover, Frank had him in a come-along hold and had slipped Forsythe's gun from his belt.

"Watch it," Forsythe groaned, "you're breaking my shoulder."

"Not really," Frank replied. "But try anything and I'll show you how close I can come to doing just that." He looked at Nancy. "Hi."

"Hello," Nancy responded. "Fancy meeting you here."

Frank was sorting through the Amos Jericho file with Nancy in her stateroom when Bess and Joe arrived.

"What's up?" Joe asked. "We got a message to meet you down here, but on the way I saw our helicopter take off. I thought they were going to wait for us."

"They were," Frank replied, his attention riveted on the photos in the Jericho file.

Nancy quickly brought the new arrivals up to date, explaining that after a brief question-and-answer session with Welsch's security staff, Forsythe had been flown back to the coast, where the police would meet him.

Joe sat on the edge of one of the beds while Bess handed him a soft drink from the stateroom's mini refrigerator. "So this guy Forsythe said he got e-mail from Amos Jericho telling him to meet him here on the *Hampton*, but Jericho never showed?"

"Right," Frank said. "That's Forsythe's story.

But he also insists that Jericho was killed three years ago in a raid in England."

"Pretty puzzling, isn't it?" Bess asked.

Frank agreed. "The connection between Trey Carter, the ticket scam, and Jericho has to turn up something." He glanced at Nancy.

"But nothing has come of it," Nancy argued.

"You caught Forsythe, and there are outstanding warrants for his arrest. That's something."

"But Forsythe being here and Jericho not being here only makes things more puzzling," she said.

"Maybe Jericho *is* here. Maybe he's as good a chameleon as—" Joe stopped what he was saying abruptly. Frank cast him a withering glance. Joe glanced down, genuinely sorry.

If Nancy noticed Joe's near blunder, she didn't mention it. But the next thing out of her mouth was what Frank had been hoping she wouldn't ask.

"So what are the two of you doing here?" she asked, fixing Frank with an intense gaze.

Frank shook his head, not happy about leaving Nancy out of the loop. "Sorry."

"I wish I'd known that before I was so generous with information on my case," Nancy said with sarcasm.

"As soon as I can tell you," Frank promised, "I will."

Frank continued flipping through the photos in the Jericho file with Nancy while Bess filled Joe in on her love life since they'd last seen each other.

A face in one of the photos caught Frank's eye. He took a closer look, not believing what he was seeing. He held the photo up.

"Joe, tell me who this is," Frank challenged.

Joe came over for a closer look. The picture showed a team of CIA agents in an airplane hangar, standing around a group of seated prisoners.

"Third man standing from the left," Frank prompted.

Recognition popped Joe's eyes open wide. "Hey, that's Norman Lowell!"

Chapter

Seventeen

NORMAN LOWELL," Nancy mused. "I remember that name. He *was* involved with Jericho—somehow. It's in one of those files, Frank." How, she wondered, do Frank and Joe know about him?

Frank shuffled through the papers in front of him. "It says here that Lowell was primarily responsible for the raid that was supposed to have killed Amos Jericho."

Nancy nodded, the details resurfacing in her mind. "That's right, and it says there, too, if I remember correctly, that Jericho and Lowell used to be partners in the CIA before Jericho was no longer needed and decided to get rich working for the other side."

Frank carefully arranged the papers into a neat

pile. He looked up at Joe. "We need to make a call."

Joe nodded.

"Wait just a minute," Nancy said sternly. "How do *you* know Norman Lowell?"

"He's the security chief for the Wedge Grove Oceanography Institute," Frank answered.

"That's where Libby McCarthy is, isn't it?" Nancy didn't wait for an answer. "And she's organized the people there for the demonstration against raising the *Titanic.*"

"That's right," Joe replied. "But how do *you* know Libby McCarthy?"

Nancy arched an eyebrow. Two could play at the secrecy game. "I saw her on the news." She glanced at Bess, who understood what Nancy was doing because she said nothing about Libby's entrance in Chicago at the museum.

"So," Nancy continued, "give it up. Tell us what you're working on."

"Can't," Frank said. "Not until we get some clearance."

Nancy had heard this from the brothers before. It usually meant they were working for the government. They were far too conscientious to talk about those cases until they had permission.

"Bummer," Nancy let out. "Well, let me know as soon as you can, okay?"

"Promise," Frank replied. He got to his feet and excused himself. Joe said good-bye—for now—and followed his brother outside.

Nancy watched the brothers go, curiosity chafing at her. She hated being left out of things.

"No," the Gray Man said. "You've fulfilled your end of the assignment. Now let it go and get back to Wedge Grove."

Frank cradled the cellular phone to his ear in frustration. He stood at the rail, watching the white-capped waves spill away from the side of the *Hampton* as the ship split the ocean. He glanced at Joe, who was standing close enough on the deck to listen in. "Is that because we'll be most useful there, or because that's where we'll be out of your way?"

"It makes no difference." The Gray Man sighed. "Frank, there are a lot of operations here that I am not at liberty to discuss with anyone. You aren't the only one who must stand in line for information. I stand there, too, though, granted, closer to the head of the line. I've only picked up some details recently myself. Trust me. When you need to know, I'll contact you."

Frank and Joe's three least favorite words— need to know—stuck out smack in the center of the Gray Man's promise. That usually meant they'd never find out.

Joe shook his head angrily and walked away.

There was nothing they could do. The Gray Man's deal was the only one on the table that would keep them in the action. Frank had no doubt that the Gray Man would ship them out if they made too many waves.

"Okay," he told the Gray Man tiredly. "You win."

"This is not about winning, Frank," the Gray Man responded. "I think you know that. I'll have the helicopter back for you in a couple of hours. Until then, stay away from Ibrahim."

"Right." Frank punched the End button on his cell phone and pocketed it. "We have time for an early dinner with Nancy and Bess before we go to the Wedge Grove boats."

"They're both going to be asking questions," Joe replied.

"Then we'll share the misery," Frank said.

Joe nodded. He looked out over the open expanse of the Atlantic Ocean. "You know, Frank, that Gray guy really burns me."

"Yeah"—Frank smiled—"I know."

"Welsch is supposed to start raising the *Titanic* four days from now," Joe said without shifting his gaze. "My bet is that's when things are going to start popping. If not, I'm the one who's going to be doing the popping."

Four days later, late in the afternoon, Welsch's engineering flotilla set about recovering the *Titanic* from the ocean bed. Nancy stood at the railing, peering over the starboard side with dozens of passengers.

Welsch's team meticulously followed the game plan that had been described on the computer-animated tapes and laser shows that had been aired all during the voyage.

The *Neptune* took up the largest amount of ocean space above the *Titanic*'s watery grave. It was not an elegant ship like the *Hampton,* but a dull metal barge with hard angles. The *Neptune* acted as a taxi and garage for the *Fearless Murphy,* Welsch's submersible, and would bear whatever Welsch's crew managed to salvage from the *Titanic.*

Winches hoisted the *Fearless Murphy* out onto the U-shaped platform at the back of the *Neptune,* then started to lower the submersible on the beginning of its two-mile drop to the ocean floor.

Ships from a handful of nations ringed the site. Nancy identified flags from the United States, the United Kingdom, France, Germany, Portugal, Spain, and Russia. It was a big news event, attracting even more attention than the most recent Mars landing.

"Any luck?" Bess stood at Nancy's elbow with a pair of binoculars pressed against her eyes.

Nancy shook her head and lowered her own binoculars. "Not so far." Both of them were scanning the crowd lining the *Hampton*'s railing for any suspicious people or actions.

Since Chauncey Forsythe had been taken into custody, two more members of Amos Jericho's old group had been evicted from the *Hampton* for traveling on forged papers. All of them swore they'd had no contact with Jericho other than the messages they'd received to meet him on board. And all three stuck to the same story—until those messages appeared, they had believed Jericho to be dead.

Nancy took out her cell phone and punched in Frank Hardy's number.

"Hello." Frank answered after nine rings. The already fuzzy connection was broken up by intermittent crackling.

"It's me," Nancy said, cupping the mouthpiece to block out the echoes of the big boats in the distance. "The *Fearless Murphy* is underwater. How are things going there?"

Helicopters from two European ships roared overhead, carrying camera crews busily filming the historic event.

"What?" Nancy cried. "I can't hear you."

"They say no news is good news," Frank repeated in a shout as the helicopter noise subsided. He sounded stressed.

Nancy swung her binoculars toward the *Gaelic Luster,* Wedge Grove's submersible carrier. The institute had put its submersible, the *Manta,* into the water an hour earlier. They planned to be in place beside the *Titanic* when the *Fearless Murphy* got there.

"Did Joe go down with the *Manta?*" Nancy asked Frank.

"There was no way to talk him out of it. We all drew straws. I probably would have gone, given the chance, but I lost."

"That depends on your perspective," Nancy commented. "If something goes wrong . . ."

"Don't think like that," Frank said.

Nancy imagined that he'd been thinking the same thing all along. "What about Norman Lowell?"

"He's here on the *Gaelic Luster*," Frank answered.

"How's he acting?"

"Business as usual, but I'm keeping an eye on him. I can't believe that the Jericho connection is a coincidence. But I also can't believe he's involved in anything suspicious either. This ex-marine is as pure as American pie."

"You mean as American as apple pie?" Nancy asked. It was not like Frank to mix his metaphors. That simply confirmed the stressful effect all this waiting was having on him.

"Yeah." Frank laughed. "What you said."

Nancy still peered through her binoculars at the *Gaelic Luster,* but couldn't locate Frank or Lowell. "Keep your back covered, Frank. My intuition tells me that once the pieces fall into place, things are going to happen very fast."

The rays of light cutting through the water had disappeared with surprising speed as the *Manta* had been swallowed by the ocean. Joe hadn't moved from his cramped corner for the last two hours. He continued to stare, transfixed, at the watery darkness, while the submersible slipped through the depths. He was beginning to wonder if he wouldn't rather be on the surface. It might not be as exciting, he thought, but at least I could walk around.

"Nervous?" Eric called from the controls.

"No," Joe fibbed, and grinned. "At least, not much."

Eric manipulated the controls with the same fluid grace he did everything. His attention centered on the sonar monitor in front of him. "I've been down several times and never quite gotten used to it."

Joe looked beyond Eric to the forward bubble window. The *Manta*'s floodlights blasted through the darkness, diluting it to a series of soft blues and casting surfaces in a greenish hue.

"Just don't go nuts on us, Twitch," Eric warned. "There's no getting out of here quickly. Even if you did get out down here—well, imagine a toothpaste tube getting stepped on and you have a pretty good idea of what would happen. The pressure on this tub, right now, is six thousand pounds per square inch."

"Now, there's a cheery thought," Mandy MacMahon said from the communications console. She wore a dark green sweatsuit against the chill. The air was kept at a low temperature to enable the electronic equipment to work at peak efficiency. She was busy writing notes in a bound notebook across her knees. Her gaze flickered back and forth from the window to the monitor screens showing different views from the outside cameras.

Without warning, a muffled thump sounded inside the sub and one of the monitor screens went dark.

"What was that?" Joe asked.

"That," Mandy explained, "was us losing one of the cameras. Evidently one of them wasn't properly protected. The pressure collapsed it."

"Like a grape," Eric elaborated, flashing an evil smile at Joe. "Nervous now?"

"I'm giving it serious consideration," Joe said. He was suddenly aware of the wet spot between his shoulder blades.

"Okay, Heckle and Jeckle," Mandy said, "it's time to be quiet. We're coming up on the *Titanic* now." She keyed in commands for the cameras on the computer array in front of her.

Joe peered through the nearby porthole but everything seemed a blur out there.

"Here," Mandy said, adjusting one of the cameras. "The telescopic lenses don't really work well this far down, but they're better than the naked eye."

Joe shuffled the tiny distance to her chair. To say there wasn't much room in the *Manta* was an understatement of great proportion. A crew of three stretched the boundaries, not only of floor space, but air space as well.

"Oh, wow," he said quietly as he got his first glimpse of the *Titanic* on the color monitor. The proud ship lay broken into two large pieces along the ocean floor. Even greatly reduced in size on the monitor, the sight took Joe's breath away.

"It's got a lot of impact when you first see it, doesn't it?" Eric asked in a reverent voice.

Joe didn't know what to say. The view cleared

as the *Manta* drew closer. He moved from the monitor back to the four-inch-thick Plexiglas porthole. The floodlights stripped the shadows and murk away to reveal the amazing hulk that had been the ocean liner everyone believed was unsinkable.

"You know," Joe said, "I've heard about the *Titanic* all my life, but I never thought I'd be on the ocean floor looking at it."

"If Walter Welsch has his way," Eric said, "everybody will be able to look at it."

Joe stared fixedly at the *Titanic* as she seemed to grow larger and larger. Eric had shown him a comparison of size specifications between the sunken ship and the *Manta,* but it hadn't prepared him for this. *It's like a cathedral,* he thought.

Breaking the spell of his reverie, Joe shifted his gaze to Mandy and Eric at the controls. "Now what?" he asked.

Mandy checked her watch. "We're about forty minutes ahead of the *Fearless Murphy.* We'll keep the cameras rolling and see what happens."

Chapter

Eighteen

"THAT'S THE *FEARLESS MURPHY*," Oliver Mac-Mahon announced with a sneer. The crew of the *Gaelic Luster* turned to survey the descending submersible that looked like nothing less than a giant prehistoric insect.

Frank watched the monitor with growing interest and anxiety. He still couldn't grasp that his brother was some two and a half miles underwater, and more than two hours away from help—if he needed it.

The concentrated silence in the *Gaelic Luster*'s command center broke only for short, direct orders. The crew's responses were instant.

The *Manta* was sending up terrific film footage of the site. Frank had heard a number of the media people congratulate the Wedge Grove video and audio technicians over and over.

"See the balloons?" Oliver asked, tapping the monitor in front of him.

Frank looked away from the sixty-inch video screen at the front of the command center to Oliver's monitor. Once he located the balloons there, he glanced back up at the huge screen to see them in even greater clarity.

Technically, they weren't balloons, but five-thousand-gallon-capacity marine lift bags filled with diesel fuel. Welsch's decision to use them was sound. Diesel fuel withstood the severe pressure of the ocean's depth and yet was lighter than water. When released, the balloons would readily float to the surface, carrying along whatever was tied to them.

The *Fearless Murphy*'s mission was to tie ten such balloons to specially designed cables that had been attached to the *Titanic*'s hull. Ballast held them down until an electronic signal from the surface was received. Then the balloons would jettison the ballast and rise, launching the front section of the ocean liner on its projected two-hour trip to the surface.

"How long will it take for the lift bags to be secured?" Frank asked.

Oliver shrugged. "An hour. Maybe more."

The idea of more waiting didn't sit well with Frank. Normally patient, he found himself growing antsy. He detested having no control over the situation almost as much as not knowing what was going on aboard the *Manta*.

He checked around the control room, taking in

all the sophisticated electronics. Global position-ing satellites kept most everything in the vicinity in view, but there were too many ships nearby to track them all.

Frank observed what a perfect setting for sabo-tage the ocean was: in the middle of nowhere, removed from any immediate restraints from the law, and with easily more than twenty ships trying to nudge their way to the front like mem-bers of a crowd waiting for a parade to start.

On the other side of the command center, Norman Lowell checked his watch, then abruptly left the room without a word.

Impulsively, Frank followed. His conversation with Nancy regarding Lowell's ties to Jericho and the CIA hammered through his mind as he drifted along in the man's wake.

Outside on the deck, Lowell made his way to a motor sailer tied up beside the *Gaelic Luster*. A handful of men joined him, quietly taking up positions on the boat and working to throw off the lines.

His curiosity turning to full-blown suspicion, Frank quietly stepped over the short distance between the *Gaelic Luster* and the motor sailer while the skeletal crew was busy getting under way. Staying low, he crawled down into the hold before any of the crew spotted him.

Frank crept forward until he was below the steering section. Over the background noise of waves slapping against the hull, Frank clearly heard Lowell's voice.

"Tell him the missiles will be waiting—just as I said they would be. But until I receive confirmation that my money is in a numbered Swiss bank account, he's not going to know where they are."

Frank peered through the porthole and spotted Lowell pacing near the front of the motor sailer. The wraparound sunglasses he wore and the cellular phone beside his face robbed the security chief of any visible expression. His voice, however, made his feelings clear.

"No!" Lowell roared. "I will *not* accept half of it. Once this thing is put into motion, there's no turning back. You just inform him that if he tries to cut my pay or chisel me on this deal, those nuclear warheads stay down there! And the *Hampton* is going down all the same. You've got ten minutes to call me back!" He punched off his phone.

Retreating back inside the hold, where Lowell wouldn't overhear him, Frank called the Gray Man on his own cellular phone.

"I'm busy, Frank," the Gray Man said. His voice sounded hollow and distant.

"If you were that busy, you wouldn't have taken this call," Frank pointed out. "You knew Joe and I were sitting on top of something big."

"Cut to the chase," the Gray Man said. "You're not the only iron I have in the fire."

"I bet not many of the others have nuclear missiles involved," Frank replied. He could tell from the dead silence that he now had the Gray

Man's complete attention. "I think I 'need to know' what's going on now."

The Gray Man paused before speaking again. "Back in the Gulf War there was a plan to use nuclear weapons against Iraq if necessary to protect Israel."

"That didn't make CNN," Frank commented.

"No. Neither did the fact that the plane bearing the nuclear weapons went down in the Atlantic Ocean only a few days after Iraq surrendered."

"Here?" Frank couldn't believe it.

"In that general vicinity, yes. The air force searched for months but never turned up anything."

"The air force," Frank repeated, his thoughts making some rather unpleasant connections.

"It *was* their plane," the Gray Man pointed out dryly. "Frank, how did you find out about the missiles?"

"I just overheard Norman Lowell demanding payment for them," Frank answered, suddenly realizing how dangerous his current position was.

"From who?"

"I didn't hear," Frank said, "but I bet I can guess. How many arms dealers do we know in the neighborhood?" Frank wandered back to the forward porthole to look at the *Hampton,* as if he might see the arms dealer Adnan Ibrahim strolling on deck.

Instead, Frank saw black puffs of smoke suddenly spring up from the *Hampton*'s decks. The smoke hung in the breeze. Then the distant, high-pitched cry of Klaxons carried across the ocean.

The *Hampton* was under attack!

The public address system aboard the *Hampton* blared out a warning only seconds after the initial explosions shook her decks. The echoes of the detonations faded away over the waves as Nancy stared into a coiling mass of black smoke and orange flames streaming from the door of a cabin no more than fifty feet from her.

"Passengers and crew of the *Hampton*," a man's deep voice ordered, "you will return to your quarters immediately. If you do not, you will be shot!"

"Up there!" one of the passengers near Nancy yelled, pointing.

Nancy looked up and spotted a trio of black-clad gunmen occupying positions on the upper decks. They carried assault rifles and suddenly opened fire high over the passengers' heads.

The barrage had its desired effect. The passengers scattered amid shouts and screams, turning the cruise liner into chaos.

Nancy ducked behind an open door leading to a companionway and held her position. She looked for Bess and found her hidden behind a table a few feet away. Nancy ran to her, crouching for cover.

"Amos Jericho!" Bess exclaimed. "He must have had more people on board."

Suddenly the mystery of Amos Jericho and his cronies fell into place for Nancy. But before she could explain to Bess, she caught sight of movement from above and saw one of the gunmen aiming a gun with a long tube for a barrel right at them.

"Move!" she told Bess, grabbing her friend's shoulder and yanking her into motion.

The tube jumped in the man's hands and Nancy heard a large object whiz by and out over the railing. Scanning the scene on the water, she saw what happened to the two-masted yacht that took the gunman's fire. In an instant the boat burst into a ball of flaming debris.

"I repeat," the voice announced over the loud-speakers. "Return to your quarters and stay there. The ship has been mined. Any efforts to resist us will result in the *Hampton*'s being blown out of the water. Evacuate all areas. A search will soon commence. If you are found outside your cabin, you will be executed."

"They're going to rob the ship!" Bess cried. She was pale and shaken. "It *is* Jericho."

Nancy remained low, watching the passengers rush by in panic-stricken waves. She shook her head. "Jericho's dead. This is someone else. Someone who knows all about Jericho and set us up to look for him. We were looking for Jericho, so they could move around the ship unnoticed.

After all, Welsch's security teams *knew* they were on the lookout for Jericho and his gang. Only they were wrong."

Only one person knew Jericho well enough to fake his presence in Chicago. The one man who would know how to create and then take advantage of such confusion was the deceased criminal's ex-partner and the man who had laid him to rest: Norman Lowell.

Nancy pulled out her cellular phone and called Frank's number. Again she took cover behind an open door, pulling Bess down beside her.

The deck around them was nearly clear and Bess was urging Nancy to move. On the fifth ring, Frank answered.

"Yeah?" Frank spoke in a whisper, his voice deep and anxious sounding.

"We're under attack," Nancy announced.

"I saw. What—"

"Lowell's behind this," Nancy said. "The people doing this are acting as if they're just going to rob the *Hampton,* but I think it's more than that. They say they've got the ship mined to explode. Why would they call so much attention to themselves? How could they hope to escape with half the world watching?

"They don't," Frank told her. "Nancy, Lowell is planning on sinking the *Hampton* as a diversion while *he* gets away."

"Gets away with what? I know Lowell's behind all this, but I don't get what all this is." Nancy flashed a look in all directions, but saw no one other than Bess.

Frank spoke even more quietly. "Nancy, listen carefully to what I'm saying. There's a man on board the *Hampton* named Adnan Ibrahim, but he's traveling under the name of Louis Adar. He's an international terrorist and arms dealer. It's his team that has seized the *Hampton*. He's in Cabin one-thirteen, A deck. That's one one three, A as in anger, deck. Get Welsch's security there immediately. It's most likely his operations base. But be care—"

"Frank!" Nancy cried. Her only answer was static, but just before the phone went dead she was sure she'd heard gunshots.

Chapter

Nineteen

"Man," Eric said in awe, "watch that baby go!"

Joe leaned over his friend's shoulder to look out the front porthole. On the other side of the broken hulk of the *Titanic,* the *Fearless Murphy* moved gracefully along the ocean floor.

As Joe watched, the *Fearless Murphy* gathered the cables of the ten marine lift bags in its robot arms and secured them to the front section of the *Titanic.*

"Once those balloons get rid of the weight that's keeping them down, the *Titanic* is going to fly right out of here," Eric predicted. "Or at least that section of the *Titanic* will."

The floodlights attached to the underbelly of the *Fearless Murphy* threw illumination in all directions, occasionally raking the *Manta.* As one of the beams glanced across its front port-hole, the glare caused the window to act as a mirror.

Reflected there, Eric and Joe saw that Mandy had turned and was holding a gun aimed at point-blank range—right at them.

"Look out!" Joe yelled.

The sharp hiss of air filled the inside of the *Manta.* Just as Joe registered that Mandy held a tranquilizer gun, he felt a sharp pain in his chest. As he fell, he plucked at the small dart that was sticking out of his shirt.

Whatever drug was in the dart, it was fast acting. Darkness swarmed over Joe, but he struggled to open his eyes. He saw through a blur that Eric had been shot before he could get up from the controls. He sat, slumped in his chair, the dart sticking out of his neck.

With all the willpower he could muster, Joe kept his eyes open, but the images before him crawled in slow motion through his brain.

Calmly, Mandy pulled Eric from his chair and dropped him beside Joe on the floor. Joe saw her sit down at the controls and felt the *Manta* lurch forward and continue moving.

Joe finally had to blink. Through a haze of disoriented vision he watched as Mandy posi-tioned the *Manta* behind the *Fearless Murphy.* The radio squawked, broadcasting orders from the pilot of the *Fearless Murphy* for the *Manta* to break off its approach.

With its robot arms caught up in the tangle of

marine lift bags, the *Fearless Murphy* remained unprotected.

Mandy guided the *Manta*'s arms toward the other submersible, and Joe heard a waterlogged sound that seemed to be metal scraping against metal. Joe struggled to lift himself so he could see the monitor. The *Fearless Murphy* seemed to sag on the screen, its arms completely collapsed on the ocean floor.

The *Manta*'s arms, however, were busy. Under Mandy's directions, they reached beyond the *Fearless Murphy* and snapped one of the balloon cables attached to the *Titanic*. The balloon in tow, the *Manta* headed off in a new direction.

The shock of what Joe was seeing hit him like a slow, rumbling roll of thunder. Summoning all his strength, Joe tried to get to his feet and stop her, but he got no further than blinking his eyes and keeping them open.

Mandy switched channels on the communications radio. Joe heard her words as if they were somehow disconnected from her body. "Recovery Base, this is Recovery Probe. I'm en route to the wreck site."

"Roger, Recovery Probe." The response was broken up by the sound of gunfire, but Joe had no problem recognizing Norman Lowell's voice.

"I hear gunfire," Mandy said.

"Not to worry," Lowell replied. "An unfortunate intruder. Taken care of. The *Hampton* is set to go down in fifteen minutes. Do you read me? Fifteen minutes until we're fabulously rich."

"I read you loud and clear, my love," Mandy crooned into the radio microphone. "I can't wait to run my fingers through all those millions Ibrahim is paying us."

Am I hallucinating? Or did I just see and hear what I think I saw and heard? The questions formed word by word in Joe's brain but no answer followed. Unable to fight the dart's drug any more, he disappeared into the inky blankness that filled his mind.

"Nancy, are you sure about this?" Welsch and his security chief, Terry Gault, stood with her on the A deck, a few doors down from Cabin 113. Down the small passageway, four more members of Welsch's security team waited for a signal.

The security team was heavily armed and all—including Welsch and Nancy—wore bullet-proof vests and headsets that kept them in constant communication with one another.

"Louis Adar is really Adnan Ibrahim," she told Welsch one more time before he took action. "Ibrahim has been identified as an international terrorist by someone I'd trust with my life."

"I suppose we're all trusting this individual," Welsch said.

"He's worth trusting." Nancy hoped that was still true. The gunshots she heard over the phone at the end of her conversation with Frank could mean the worst. Frank could be wounded—or killed. When she'd tried calling him back, the line was dead.

"If your friend is wrong . . ." Welsch left the rest unsaid.

Nancy understood the danger. Welsch's team had confirmed the presence of bombs in strategic locations aboard the *Hampton*. If she was wrong, everyone on the ship might go down in the resulting explosions. But she knew she was right.

"Okay, Terry," Welsch said to his security chief. "Let's take back our ship."

Gault gave a tight nod and issued hand signals to his crew. The eight security people raced through the passageway toward the targeted cabin. Welsch let them pass, but stayed close behind them, as Nancy kept watch.

In the momentary silence before they blasted the door open, Nancy heard the sound of footsteps. She flattened herself against the wall, knowing if she yelled out a warning to the security team, she'd warn whoever was approaching as well.

The man who came around the corner wasn't one of the security staff; he was one of Ibrahim's men. He spotted the security team and started to raise his rifle.

Working on sheer adrenaline, Nancy stepped forward to halt the intruder. The gunman saw her coming and prepared to shove her away. Using his weight and momentum against him, however, Nancy executed a clean throw that sent the man crashing into the wall and then to the floor.

He collapsed just as the door to Cabin 113 blew.

Nancy turned in time to see the last of the security team and Welsch storming into the cabin. Gunfire quickly ripped through the passageway and was over.

Nancy took a deep breath and slowly counted to ten before she started walking toward the cabin. About halfway there, Welsch emerged.

"It's over, Nancy," he said, reaching out to take her hand. "All the detonation controls were in the room, and they have all been shut down.

"Way to go," he said as he raised his other hand in a high-five. They slapped hands victoriously.

Welsch suddenly pulled away as he caught sight of the unconscious terrorist on the floor. His eyebrows rose. "You *are* a talented girl."

It's good to be appreciated, Nancy thought. "What about Ibrahim?"

"Gault's got him cuffed, and he's being escorted to the brig right now," Welsch answered.

"And his men on the rest of the ship?" she persisted.

"They'll soon find out that they've stepped into a trap themselves." Welsch flipped open a cellular phone and said no more than five or six crisp words into it. He then took Nancy's arm and led her outside.

Four armed military helicopters suddenly appeared.

"I don't think we're going to have a problem convincing the others that resistance is futile. Do you?" Welsch gave Nancy a broad smile.

"No," Nancy said, but she couldn't find the heart to smile yet—not until she knew that Frank and Joe were okay.

Joe might have preferred being unconscious to having the headache that pounded at his temples. He barely opened his eyes, wanting to get his bearings before alerting Mandy that he was alive and had regained consciousness.

Mandy was still seated at the controls, staring at the screen in front of her.

Joe raised himself up, refusing to be daunted by the pain and grogginess that threatened to overcome him. When his eyes finally focused, he saw that in place of the *Titanic* lay the broken fuselage of an airplane with the United States Air Force insignia emblazoned on its side.

The *Manta*'s thrusters suddenly sprang to life and the submersible shifted its position. Joe couldn't see any more from where he was. He had to get up.

Joe silently crawled the three or four steps to bring Mandy's monitor into view without giving himself away. Mandy seemed lost in concentration, and Joe considered simply pinning her to the chair and demanding answers. But the image on the monitor's screen captured his attention.

As he watched, Mandy guided the submersible's robot arms into the cargo hold of the plane.

Then she adjusted the controls to enlarge the monitor's image. The arms were reaching for a crate. Although the scene was dark and murky, Joe had no trouble making out the yellow and black triangular nuclear warning markings on its side.

Mandy didn't quite manage to tie the balloon's cable to the crate on the first try. The robot arms moved slowly, and the activity stirred up whirlpools from the ocean floor.

That's the prize Mandy said was worth millions to the right buyer, a buyer by the name of Adnan Ibrahim, Joe thought.

Whether from the realization of Mandy and Lowell's treachery or from the aftereffects of the drug, Joe's heart began to pound wildly. An involuntary groan escaped from his lips.

Mandy twisted around in the chair with the tranquilizer gun at the ready. She fired as Joe beat back rising nausea and lunged for her.

The dart whisked past Joe's ear and pinged off the bulkhead behind him. In seconds Joe pulled himself into position and took a swing. His fist caught her on the jaw, and she was out.

Hanging on to his consciousness, Joe licked his dry lips and struggled to focus on the command console in front of him. The training Eric had given him seemed lost in the cotton filling his brain. He managed to cut power to the thrusters, then open the robot arm's claw to release the marine lift bag.

With the *Manta* sitting idle, he took one more

look around to see if there was anything else to take care of. He picked up Mandy's tranquilizer gun and then hit the ballast release.

The *Manta* began its steady rise to the surface. Joe closed his eyes and tried not to be sick. Even if Mandy came to while he was out again, she couldn't stop the sub. They were on a one-way trip.

The gunman and Frank saw each other at the same time.

The man lifted his weapon and fired as Frank dropped his cell phone and dove forward to cut the distance between himself and the man. Frank came up out of a roll and swung a backhanded hammer blow to the man's temple.

The man partially dodged the swing. He let go of his rifle and slipped a thick-bladed knife from a holster on his hip.

Frank continued to take the offensive, wary that a defensive fight against the man and his knife in such close quarters would not turn out well for him. Frank aimed a punch and stepped into it with all his weight behind it.

The air went out of the man in a *whoosh*. Frank kicked the knife out of his hand, then finished the fight with a front snap kick. The man went down.

Picking up the cellular phone, Frank discovered that he'd lost the connection to Nancy. He dialed the Gray Man's number as he stooped to pick up the assault rifle for protection.

The phone rang once before the Gray Man answered. "The *Hampton* is under attack," Frank said as he ran up to the deck.

"I've got the situation in hand," the Gray Man replied. "A helicopter team has already been dispatched. I wasn't caught entirely off guard by the turn of events. Where are you?"

Frank came up onto the top deck cautiously. "I'm on a motor sailer that left the *Gaelic Luster* only a few minutes ago," Frank answered.

"Everything down there is chaos," the Gray Man advised. "You're going to have to do better than that if we're going to find you."

Spotting the emergency kit bolted to the wall beside the stairway, Frank said, "I *can* do better than that." He scanned the horizon and found the four military choppers winging toward the *Hampton.*

"I can see your helicopters," Frank said. "That means they can see me."

"If they know where to look."

Frank reached into the emergency kit and took out the flare gun and spare cartridges. "I'll make it easy for them." The fat cartridges were color coded for red smoke. "Tell them to look for the red cloud."

"Is Norman Lowell there with you?"

"Yes." Frank armed the pistol while cradling the phone on his shoulder.

"I'd rather he didn't get away," the Gray Man said. "He was something of a surprise. I'd found out Ibrahim knew about the missiles from an

American source, but I hadn't identified who yet."

"I'll see what I can do about delaying him. Send someone to get him." He disconnected the phone, aimed the flare gun, and pulled the trigger. A red tornado rose into the sky. He aimed again, at the deck, and embedded another flare. The two red storms mingled on the breeze.

The flare's smoke burned the back of Frank's throat as he put in the final cartridge.

A man suddenly came around the cabin, his rifle aimed at Frank.

Frank leveled the flare gun and pulled the trigger. The flare slammed against the man's Kevlar vest, shooting out smoke and sparks and knocking the man down.

After a second, the stricken gunman was on his feet running away, while struggling to get out of his very hot vest.

Tossing the useless flare pistol aside, Frank took up his borrowed assault rifle. His mind turned to Lowell and he ran flat out toward the bow of the boat, where he had last seen the renegade.

Before he rounded the cabin, he spotted one of the European news helicopters descending toward the motor sailer. Just below, at the prow of the boat, Lowell stood, seemingly transfixed.

The helicopter stabilized, and from its cargo bay a rolled rope ladder tumbled out, unfurling in the wind.

Lowell stretched himself as tall as possible and

reached for the bottom rung of the ladder. He missed by inches. The helicopter pulled away to make adjustments and try another pass.

Frank knew if Lowell managed to get off the boat and onto a foreign ship friendly to him, the Gray Man's teams wouldn't have a chance of getting him.

The motor sailer bobbed on the turbulent ocean, making Lowell's chances of catching the rope ladder less than ideal, but he only needed a hint of success and he'd be gone.

As both Lowell and Frank watched, two military helicopters with US markings bore down on them. The cavalry was coming.

Frank returned his gaze to the prow just in time to see the rope ladder smack against Lowell's hand. The ex-marine, ex-CIA agent grasped the rung and raised a foot to start his climb.

Frank drew the assault rifle to his shoulder and took aim. Leaving the weapon on full auto, he emptied the clip in a single burst. Moving the barrel only slightly, he swept the rope ladder about four feet above Lowell's head.

The bullets sliced through the rope, and the ladder gracefully fell like a net over Lowell. He looked like a captured animal trapped in a net. But the ladder was easily thrown off, and, raising his rifle, Lowell was still the hunter.

Frank saw the fullness of Lowell's rage on his face as the man took aim and fired.

As Frank flipped backward into cover, the

bullets ate into the side of the cabin where he'd been standing. "It's over, Lowell!" Frank shouted. He reloaded the assault rifle.

"You won't shoot me!" Lowell yelled back.

"Maybe not," Frank admitted. Then he pointed at the military helicopters. "But they will."

Lowell's escape copter had already fled the scene, abandoning him.

Reluctantly, the man let his rifle drop, then placed his hands on his head.

Frank breathed a sigh of relief—too soon. A splash erupted from the surface of the ocean. Lowell had jumped.

Half a dozen similar splashes followed as five armed Navy Seals jumped from the hovering aircraft.

Frank waited before he breathed another sigh of relief, right on time.

Chapter

Twenty

Nancy, Bess, Frank, and Joe sat in Walter Welsch's private quarters on the *Hampton* with their host early that evening, savoring their quiet security. The Gray Man's crews had cleared the ocean liner of the bombs left by Adnan Ibrahim's group, but the news reporters still haunted the passageways, trying to get an interview from anyone who knew anything about the day's events.

"So you were never really going to raise the *Titanic*," Nancy stated.

The billionaire shook his rather handsomely disheveled head. "The government asked me to cooperate with them in creating this screen."

"Screen? What were they hiding?" Bess asked.

Since the Hardys and Bess and Nancy had all been acting separately during the crisis, they all had stories to tell and each lacked certain pieces of information.

"The plane with the nuclear weapons had been on a secret military mission during the Gulf War," Welsch explained, "but the war ended before the plan was carried out. On the way back to the States, the plane went down. The government didn't want the public to know about it. Public security and all.

"They knew the plane had gone down somewhere in this region. If they'd sent a team in to salvage it, they would have attracted all kinds of unwanted attention. I was supposed to attempt to raise the *Titanic,* but fail." Welsch shook his head. "It was a dilemma for me, you see, because I believe that no one has any business raising the *Titanic* after all these years."

"So your phony attempt to raise the ship got all the attention," Joe said, "instead of the government's attempt to salvage the missiles."

"Clever," Frank interjected.

Welsch nodded. "It could have worked out pretty well, too. . . ."

Nancy finished his sentence for him. "If Lowell and Mandy hadn't been after the nuclear weapons as well."

"Having been in the military and the CIA, those two knew how to blind government intelligence agencies. No one had a clue what they were up to. In fact, they were considered highly trustworthy." Welsch chuckled and shook his head.

"Makes you wonder about the phrase 'military intelligence.'"

"But how did Mandy and Lowell know about the bombs?" Bess asked.

"Mandy MacMahon," Joe said with some disgust.

"Joe, someday you'll learn not to judge a book by its cover," Frank chided, though he was smiling.

"Yeah, what a mistake that was," Joe confessed. "Between all this work and the hours I spent trying to get her to notice me, I've wasted my whole vacation."

"I wouldn't call what you did on board the *Manta* today a waste," Welsch commented. "In fact, if it weren't such a high-level secret, I bet you'd be getting some kind of medal from the President himself."

"Please, Walter," Bess said with a groan, "his head is big enough as it is. You'll make him unbearable to live with." She held up her hand. "I'm not finished. So, this Mandy knew, but how did she find out?"

Frank took up the story. "She was in the Air Force until a few months ago. It turns out that she was actually a member of the reconnaissance team searching for the missing plane. Bad luck— she found it first and decided to keep the location to herself. She reported the plane's position as being just a few miles away—close enough to fool any satellite or sonar investigation, but far enough away that the government submersible sent to retrieve it was hopelessly lost. Then she got out of the service and went to Wedge Grove to make her plans. She found a kindred spirit in the institute's security chief, former CIA agent Norman Lowell."

"A larcenous kindred spirit," Nancy observed.

Joe raised his glass in a salute. "Lowell must have arranged the attack on us our first night."

"It helped convince Libby McCarthy to go through with the demonstration, and, if you'll excuse me"—Frank nodded at Welsch—"it was part of an attempt to frame you—at least in Libby's mind."

"That's why he faked the security tapes showing one of your employees sabotaging equipment at the institute," Joe continued, "and blew up the boat the morning after we arrived. He was trying to keep pressure on Libby, make her think you were a bad guy."

Nancy caught the sad expression on Welsch's face as he listened. He must be wondering if things can go back to the way they were with Libby, she thought.

"Later," Joe said, "Lowell destroyed the security tapes because anyone with an ounce of experience in computer-generated images would have known they were fake."

Welsch looked up at Nancy. "How does Amos Jericho fit into all this?"

"That," Nancy said, "we have to guess at. Of course, Jericho wasn't really involved at all. He did die three years ago. But it wasn't coincidental that Lowell led the raid that killed him. He knew Jericho, and he knew how to get in touch with the people Jericho had employed. Evidently he sent for them to use as yet another cover for his own operation."

"What about Trey Carter?" the billionaire asked.

"Unless Mandy or Lowell confesses," Frank said, "we have to speculate on that, too. The way I see it, Lowell must have hired Carter to steal the cruise tickets. Then he tipped off the radio station by having people call in claiming that they'd been offered the tickets."

Welsch shook his head. "And all just to draw attention to his cover?"

"Yes," Nancy agreed. "That way your security staff would be looking for Jericho and his gang instead of someone like Ibrahim. Jericho was a false lead, just like the one you were constucting for the government."

Welsch fixed her with his gaze. "But you said Jericho was identified in Chicago. You said you even had him on tape."

"Mistaken identity," Nancy answered. "We figure that Ibrahim, who was buying the missiles from Lowell and Mandy, agreed to kill Carter. Ibrahim, after all, is known for his disguises. He probably just disguised himself as Jericho—or, rather, as Jericho in disguise as an alien, of all things—and then he killed Carter."

Welsch leaned back in his chair, staring at the

blank television screen mounted in the wall. He sighed. "I'm bushed. My brain feels as if it's been scrambled. In a couple of hours, I've got to go in front of dozens of television reporters and announce that the *Titanic* won't be coming up."

"At least the government will have recovered the nuclear weapons by then," Frank put in.

Welsch nodded glumly.

Nancy leaned toward Welsch and spoke quietly. "Before you talk to the reporters, you might want to tell someone else the news."

Welsch's face quickly changed from glum to confused to hopeful. "Libby." Welsch rubbed his chin. "You're a woman. Do you think she'll understand?"

"I don't *think* she will," Nancy replied, "I *know* she will."

Welsch pushed himself up from his chair. "If you'll excuse me, I have a telephone call to make."

His guests began to stand up to leave.

"No, no," Welsch said. "Sit, sit. I'll use the phone in my office. I'd love to stay and have dinner with you, but I'm hoping for an invitation to dine aboard the *Gaelic Luster* tonight. Stay as long as you want. Help yourselves to anything you want—videos, soft drinks—anything from room service." He waved and was out the door in no time flat.

A sly smile crept across Bess's face. "How does it feel to be dumped by a billionaire, Nancy?"

"Once and for all, Bess Marvin," Nancy spoke

sternly, "there is nothing—and never was anything—between Walter Welsch and myself."

Bess just winked at her best friend. "How about we go check out the dining room, Joe? We've got a couple of hours before the dance."

"I'm there!" Joe exclaimed, getting up to go. "See you guys. Don't get into any trouble now."

The room grew very silent after Bess and Joe set off.

"What are you thinking?" Nancy asked Frank.

"Not much," he answered. "Just kind of letting go of it all."

"No more excitement and no more mysteries," Nancy lamented.

"For now," Frank said.

"What are you and Joe going to do?"

"Go finish up—or rather start—the vacation we'd planned at Wedge Grove."

"What about tonight?" Nancy asked.

Frank lifted a curious eyebrow. "What about tonight?" he echoed suspiciously.

"Despite the fact that the *Titanic* will rest at the bottom of the ocean, at least for the time being, there's still going to be a Raise the *Titanic* dance tonight."

"Are you asking me to go to the dance with you, Drew?"

"Definitely not," Nancy said in feigned shock. "However, I am pointing out the opportunity you have for asking me!"